# Praise for *Skin and Bones*

"*Skin and Bones* is a unique and engaging portrait of young people with eating disorders. Sherry Shahan does a fantastic job of accurately and non-judgmentally shining a light on the cognitive distortions that accompany eating disorders, and the behaviours that can manifest through them, without losing sight of the humanity of her characters. Protagonist Jack doesn't want to be sick, but his eating disorder has a tight hold on his world. These seemingly contradictory elements are true for many people who suffer from an eating disorder. Congratulations to Shahan for accurately representing how eating disorders may manifest in youth, and for reminding us all that eating disorders affect men and boys as well as women. *Skin and Bones* is compulsively readable, touching, and surprisingly humorous. Well done!"—*Jackie Grandy, Outreach & Education Coordinator, The National Eating Disorder Information Centre*

"Shahan has crafted a fast-moving story of addiction and first love that—refreshingly—will appeal to male readers, who don't find themselves regularly represented in eating-disorder-treatment-and-recovery fiction."—*Booklist*

"The writing is simple and accessible, and Bones' warped self-image is effectively conveyed..."—*Bulletin of the Center for Children's Books*

"Misconceptions about eating disorders being a 'female' disease often perpetuate strong feelings of shame in males with an eating disorder. This shame often results in the denial of the eating disorder and/or reluctance to seek treatment. Male eating disorders are on the rise. A 2007 study by Harvard Medical School found that 25% (not the traditionally stated 10–15%) of study participants with anorexia and bulimia were male. An estimated 40% of those with binge eating disorder are male. It is of the utmost importance to raise awareness of this issue, *Skin and Bones*, does that in a non-threatening way. It reminds us to look for the warning signs of low self-esteem, depression, anxiety, feeling of worthlessness, feelings of self-loathing, and the need for acceptance. The author describes the difficulty for expressing emotion in very real terms. *Skin and Bones* addresses a topic much ignored in an open and honest story."—*Sharon M. Glynn, LPN; Director of Programming, The Alliance For Eating Disorders Awareness*

"Shahan tackles eating disorders in a fast-paced, contemporary coming-of-age novel…A quick read with a worthy message: We are all recovering from something, and the right companions can help you heal. The wrong ones can kill you."—*Kirkus Reviews*

"The plot is well paced and develops quickly…"—*School Library Journal*

# SKIN and
# BONES

# SKIN and BONES

# BONES

## Sherry Shahan

**ALBERT WHITMAN & COMPANY**
CHICAGO, ILLINOIS

Library of Congress Cataloging-in-Publication Data

Shahan, Sherry.
Skin & bones / Sherry Shahan.
pages cm
Summary: Jack, who is sixteen and has anorexia, spends the summer in an
eating disorder ward for teenagers and befriends both his overweight roommate
and a dangerously thin dancer.
ISBN 978-0-8075-7401-0
[1. Anorexia nervosa—Fiction. 2. Eating disorders—Fiction.
3. Friendship—Fiction.
4. Hospitals—Fiction.] I. Title. II. Title: Skin and bones.
PZ7.S52784Sk 2014
[Fic]—dc23  2013028442

Printed in the United States of America
10  9  8  7  6  5  4  3  2  1  LB  20  19  18  17  16  15  14

Cover design by Nick Tiemersma.

For more information about Albert Whitman & Company,
visit our web site at www.albertwhitman.com.

*For Krise and Kyle, daughters divine*

# 1

To Jack Plumb room number 19 B looked like an ordinary college dorm. Two beds, two dressers, two desks, two chairs. Cinder block walls painted eggshell. If the linoleum ever had color, it had long since been scuffed off. Even the bedspreads appeared to be sickly.

Unfortunately Jack knew the sorry truth. The room was in the corner wing of a hospital that treated all kinds of patients—in the wing that housed a program for people with major food issues, the Eating Disorders Unit (EDU).

"Welcome to the loony foodie bin," said the orderly. His name was Bruno, and he was muscle-bound with a square head and a bushy unibrow.

Jack guessed he was trying to ease the tension. "Uh, thanks."

Jack hefted his ratty duffle onto the bed that had to be his. The other one was unmade and a poster hung above it with Rachael Ray in a skin-tight, low-cut T-shirt with *Yum-O!*

written across her chest.

"And Jack," the guy said, "group therapy is at ten o'clock."

"Got it."

"The rest of the gang is in the dayroom watching TV if you're interested."

"Thanks, but I think I'll unpack," Jack said, unzipping his duffle.

He hoped he wouldn't have much interaction with Unibrow, especially after the thoroughly embarrassing pat down an hour ago with Jack in a flimsy cotton gown with ties in back. Unibrow's job was to make sure no one smuggled contraband into the hospital. And that didn't mean cigarettes, drugs, or razor blades taped between butt cheeks.

"Damn," Jack had mumbled after Unibrow discovered the ankle weights he'd stashed in what he'd thought was a secret compartment in his duffle.

Unibrow had dropped the weights into a wastebasket with an ominous clunk.

Jack had tried to act like he didn't care. But he cared a ton, *damn it!* Ankle weights turned squats into relentless fat burners.

Unibrow had taken the standard vitals: temperature, blood pressure, height, and weight. Jack had sucked all the air from the claustrophobic four-by-four of a room before stepping lightly as possible onto the old-school mechanical scale with sliding weights.

"One-hundred-two and nine-ounces." Unibrow had scribbled on Jack's chart. "You can get dressed now."

Jack had grabbed his sweats and let out the breath he'd been holding. He'd lost four ounces.

. . . . . . . . . .

Jack unpacked sweatshirts, sweatpants, thick athletic socks, wool beanies. He wore them to encourage his body to reach a temperature hot enough to melt solids. No matter what anyone said, sweat was nothing but liquid fat. That's why it smelled like rancid bacon grease. As conundrums go, sweat was also his most private and trusted confidante.

His sister had helped him pack for the extended incarceration, because their mom was upset about his being away for six weeks. The length of time of the program was designed to accommodate teens over summer vacation.

Jack had reluctantly agreed to the program, because it wasn't one of those lock-down facilities. Also because his school counselor had said, "If you keep going like this, you'll end up in a coma." Bully tactics.

Jack's parents blamed themselves for his eating disorder, convinced it was caused by something they did or didn't do. "I'm sorry I made you eat those disgusting strained carrots when you were a baby," his mom once said.

"Seriously?" his older sister had put in. "I ate them too and I'm not skinny."

Most of the time his dad avoided discussions like these.

Here's the truth: Jack didn't blame his family for his

problems with food. He liked his parents okay. His workaholic dad sold car insurance, house insurance, life insurance, and had memorized how much his clients were worth dead—he was the kind of guy who'd give you the shirt off his back, then offer to wash and iron it. His mom ran the household like an executive—shopping, cooking, cleaning, paying bills. Any spare time was spent raising money for the homeless shelter.

"Try to get better," his sister had said while folding the Darth Vader sweatshirt she'd picked up for him at a garage sale.

Jack had looked away, feeling guilty, knowing what Jill meant. *It would be great if we could go out for pizza sometime. Maybe even sneak a beer, you know, like normal teenagers.* He wasn't sure what she had meant by *better*, but he was hoping to come home less obsessed about what he would or wouldn't eat.

Jack had opened up for a hug, holding her tight, even though he'd known he'd be absorbing calories from the vanilla extract she dabbed behind her ears, praying the huddle would produce enough sweat to burn it off.

Jill had bought him paperbacks from a used bookstore, cheesy novels with sexy women on the cover. As if she thought he should have a different date every night to keep him company. No way these books were safe to read. People ate all kinds of things while curled up on a recliner— smearing grease and leaving crumbs that an unsuspecting person might ingest. Used books were definitely a slippery proposition. "I love you, weirdo," she'd said. "Don't do anything stupid."

"Like I'll have a chance," he'd said. "It's a hospital."

Jack had sobbed a little. More leakage. He couldn't wait to weigh himself.

"No laxatives."

"I stopped using them after, you know—" he'd paused, embarrassed all over again remembering the day he didn't make it to the bathroom in time.

"No diuretics either," she'd said. "No ipecac syrup. No enemas. And, please, promise me, no fingers down the throat."

"No fun!"

They'd both laughed, knowing how crazy this sounded. Then he'd reminded her, "I don't do that stuff anyway."

"I mean it," she'd said, suddenly serious.

"I know."

And he meant it too. No one *likes* to be sick. Any more than a heroin addict *likes* sticking a needle in his arm or a chronic masturbator *likes* having all that free time on his hands.

Jack finished hanging his clothes in the closet, pointing neck holes in the same direction. Everything was black so he didn't have to worry about coordinating colors. Next he checked out the boxy bathroom. It had a toilet, no urinal, and a mirror over a porcelain sink. A toothbrush and tube of toothpaste stood in a plastic mug, crowding a shelf with a brush matted with black hair. Next to the mug, shoelaces hung over a small box of hemorrhoid cream.

Jack decided to shower off the smog and exhaust from the drive through the San Fernando Valley. He undressed quickly, annoyed because he couldn't see below his chest in the mirror without overturning the waste can and balancing precariously on its circular bottom.

Jack was proud of his body, especially the six-pack stretched tightly across his abdomen. He stared into the glass and flexed a bicep, roughly the size of his wrist, and wondered if he'd ever be brave enough to get naked in front of a girl.

Then he blushed because he was really thinking, *A skinny girl like me. But with curves and bumps where curves and bumps are supposed to be.*

Jack stepped down from the waste can. He looked around for a scale, alarmed when he didn't see one. *I'll have to ask a nurse about it*, he thought, suddenly shivering. He cranked the faucet in the shower. For a moment he considered getting his sneakers so he wouldn't have to touch the floor of the shower. Maybe the gift shop sold flip-flops.

He left the bathroom door open. "As per EDU rule number one hundred," he muttered sarcastically.

An open door was supposed to discourage purging, at least from the two most obvious orifices. Jack never threw up, unless he had the flu and except for that time he got food poisoning from his sister's undercooked meatloaf. Anorexics got such a bad rap; people often assumed they threw up after eating. Although he'd met an anorexic girl in his last therapy group who'd stuck her finger down her throat after her mom forced her to eat a cup of vegetable broth.

He scrubbed with a loofah and dribbled pee the color of root beer. It didn't smell so hot either. Dehydration. But he never drank water until after he weighed. An eight-ounce glass of water weighed just that. Eight ounces. Eight glasses per day? It didn't take an Einstein to calculate.

Jack toweled off and grabbed his sweatpants and Darth Vader sweatshirt. Because it was from his sister and somewhat comforting, it gave him enough confidence to venture into the corridor and look for a nurse.

He stopped the first woman he saw. "Excuse me," he said. "My bathroom doesn't have a scale."

"Jack, isn't it?" she said, her voice chirpy. "I'm Nancy, head nurse on the ward. How's it going?"

Nancy looked near his mom's age and could stand to lose the same twenty pounds. She had an old-school perm, but on her it didn't look too bad.

"Do you have digital scales?" he asked. "Calibrated to a quarter ounce?"

"Sorry, but you're only weighed once a week while you're in here."

Jack felt familiar rumbles of panic. In the last four years he'd known his weight day by day, sometimes hour by hour. After waking up, before peeing, after peeing, before breakfast, after breakfast, before jogging…

He slumped against the wall. "No one told me."

"Have you gotten your menus?" she asked, changing the subject.

He shook his head. "No."

"I'll print copies and bring them to your room," she said. "You're in nineteen-B, right? With David. They put you two together because you're the only guys. You'll get along great."

Jack retreated to his cave, feeling sick to his stomach. Really sick. He just made it to the edge of the toilet, bending over, head between his knees. He willed myself not to throw up. The staff would think he did it on purpose.

When the woozy feeling passed, he went to his spartan desk. The other one was jam-packed with magazines, cookbooks, and a forty-eight ounce mug that said *Don't Leave Home Without It*. The bulletin board was covered with recipes torn from newspapers.

Jack scanned the recipes, stricken by a case of the dreads so thick they rolled through the room. For the next six weeks he'd be stuck with a roommate who was obsessed with eating. Which confirmed what Jack already knew—agreeing to check in to this rehab for food losers was a mistake.

# 2

Jack hit the floor and fired off push-ups until he thought he'd pass out. The spinning behind his eyes felt good. He'd gotten by with a half grapefruit (35 calories) at breakfast, because his mom was such an emotional wreck before driving him to the hospital. She didn't argue over the half cup of oatmeal (110 calories), which he dumped in the sink before polishing off the last of his red M&M's from the night before. For a year, M&M's had been his go-to food when life got sucky.

Jack plopped on his bed with *Weight Watchers* magazine. He was just getting into an article called "You Are What You Eat," when a short, squat guy with a slightly dangerous body mass came in. He reminded Jack of the kind of guy who'd been shaving since kindergarten. Jack didn't even own a razor.

"What's cookin'?" the guy asked in a voice too big for the four walls.

He even looked like a food addict. "Not much."

Jack noticed his glasses—wide, black frames. Buddy Holly knock-offs. His shirt was splattered with pin-size dots. It looked like he'd been sprayed with Worcestershire sauce. His belly jiggled inside loose-fitting pants with a drawstring waist. If the vertical black and white stripes were supposed to make him look tall and thin, they weren't working.

"According to my chart," the guy said, moving to his side of the room. "I'm a seventeen-year-old compulsive overeater named David Kowlesky. But you can call me Lard."

Lard set a *Toy Story 3* lunch box on his desk. Buzz Lightyear and Woody stared up with fixed eyebrows. Lard stretched out a beefy hand.

Jack shook it, feeling his own hand disappear in the grip. "Did you say Lard?"

"As in, fat-tub-of..."

That seemed a bit insensitive for a program claiming to boost one's self esteem.

"I learned a long time ago that if you're fat and don't give yourself a nickname, someone else will," Lard said. "I sneaked a looked at your chart. Jack Plumb. Sixteen-year-old male. Five-foot-eleven. One-hundred-three pounds."

Jack didn't ask how he had access to medical files.

"Anorexic. Sometimes in denial, sometimes not. Promising candidate for the program," Lard said all official-like. "Family intact. Both your parents live under the same roof?"

Jack nodded. "Yeah."

"My dad is some guy who had sex with my mom and she doesn't remember who he was because it was during her hippie-druggie-commune period," Lard said. "And the reason I eat half a dozen pizzas at a time while glued to the Food Channel is because it fills the hole in my gut from not knowing my sperm donor."

Why would this guy be spewing his family history now? Jack figured it was his standard bullshit.

"I bet your parents have screaming matches that turn into knock-down fights and your neighbors call the cops."

Jack shrugged. "They hardly even argue."

"They must be repressed." Lard stuck a finger in his mug and flicked water. "Jack Plumb, I hereby christen you Toothpick."

Jack blotted his face before his skin could soak it up. He needed a minute to think. Toothpicks had two functions— to spear food or pick teeth. Having a nickname so closely associated with eating wouldn't cut it. "What about Bones? As in, skin-and—"

"I like it," Lard said. He sat at his desk, combat boots propped on the windowsill. "This place has about a million rules designed to—and I quote—keep us safe. Like, what are we? Fucking nine-year-olds? We can't even shut the bathroom door to take a dump. You know the fart fan? It's disconnected so they can *listen*. Talk about sick."

"They want to make sure we aren't tossing our cookies," Jack—aka Bones—said.

"Do I look like I spend a lot of time throwing up?"

"Not really."

"They go through our trash too. Patients find all kinds of places to get rid of what they've eaten. I call them Vomitus Interruptus." Lard studied Bones. "Just so you know, I'm not into that crap. If you are, that's your business. But I don't want to hear it, and don't ever let me smell it. Let me see your knuckles."

Bones held up his hands to show he didn't have scars from sticking his fingers down his throat.

"You wouldn't believe what they do with chocolate laxatives," Lard said. "Put them in brownies—shave it over ice cream."

Bones believed it. He'd gone through boxes of them since that fateful day in the sixth grade. That was another reason he'd agreed to check into the program. He didn't want to spend the rest of his life worrying about soiling his skivvies.

"I'm learning to cook while I'm here," Lard said. "I help the chef in the kitchen. Gumbo, a real chef. Not one of those fast-food poseurs in a Pillsbury hat."

"Isn't it sketchy being around food like that?"

"No, man, it's just the opposite. There's something about cooking that keeps me from wanting to eat everything in sight."

Bones tried to follow his logic. He hadn't thought that highly of food since he was ten-and-a-half and a store clerk handed him jeans labeled *Husky*. "Try these on for size," she'd said. Until then, he'd thought he was going through a growth spurt. But the clerk must've known better because *Husky* fit just right, as reinforced by a triangle of full-length mirrors.

And that's how it had started.

With one lousy remark.

That was the first time he'd tried to lose a few pounds. He tested the Grapefruit Diet, Atkins Diet, South Beach Diet, 24-Hour Miracle Diet, Cabbage Soup Diet, Fat Smash Plan, the Master Cleanse. He listened to crashing waves on a CD called *Thirty-Day Subliminal Weight Loss Plan: Lose Fat While Your Unconscious Mind Does the Work*, which made him want to pee constantly.

"How long's your sentence?" Bones asked.

"A month this time," Lard said. "Three months last summer. Entered the program with type two diabetes—on insulin and everything. Lost over one hundred pounds, man."

Bones couldn't imagine that. "Why'd you come back?"

"Sort of like a refresher course, and, like I said, I like working in the kitchen."

There was a loud knock on the mostly open door.

"It's open," Lard deadpanned.

Nancy peeked in. "GTs in twenty minutes, guys. Don't be late."

"Group therapy," Lard said after she left. "It's all about *feelings*."

Bones knew what GT meant. He'd suffered through

every type of therapy session: Art Therapy Groups, Peer Group, Body Image Groups, Creative Expression Groups, Imaginative Movement Groups. Skill Training Group was a catchall that included anger management (punching bags), relaxation (meditation), and social training (playing cards). He'd endured endless lectures by so-called experts, who insisted patients begin every sentence with *I feel...*

*Food isn't the issue,* they all droned on. *It's about seeking perfection in an imperfect world and the need to be in control of one's destiny.*

"And be careful what you say around here. The walls have ears." Lard swung his stubby legs to the floor and grabbed a journal off his desk. "Come on, it's time to meet the rest of the tribe."

# 3

The dayroom was about as inviting as a mausoleum. It had a basic worn couch, mismatched chairs, shelves with ancient board games, tattered paperbacks, plastic chess pieces. Folding chairs were arranged in a haphazard circle.

Bones stood by a window staring at the street below. A metro bus gusted by on the street, followed by a blur of cyclists. An ambulance turned into the emergency entrance, reminding him that the program took up only one wing of the ten-story building. Typical type hospital activities went on everywhere else.

"Everyone gets a journal," Lard said, choosing a folding chair. "It's a ritual."

"Can't wait."

"Look at me," Lard said. He leaned across the room and thrust his face at Bones. "What do you see?" Bones saw brown eyes behind glasses that were so uncool they were actually cool and a face that held the secrets of being pockmarked. The usual result of excessive amounts of sugar and fat.

"There are basically two kinds of people in here," Lard said. "Losers with eating disorders, and me. I like to eat. Food tastes good. It's what keeps me alive. But I don't overdo it anymore. Since you're one type and I'm another—we should probably make a pact right here and now."

"Yeah?"

"You don't mess with my shit and I won't mess with your shit."

It made sense. "Cool shit."

"We're gonna get along just fine."

A girl in flannel pj's and bunny slippers waddled in. Her face was the color of hot cocoa with more milk than chocolate. Her hair and eyes, espresso beans. Her pierced eyebrow looked like it was bleeding.

"Hey, Teresa," Lard said. "You doing okay?"

PJ Girl plunked down so hard her chair skidded. "Some days are the pits," she said, wiping her nose on her sleeve. "Some are the shits."

Bones tried not to stare but her belly was enormous. It overflowed around her waist to her back, making her look like she had an extra butt.

A second girl came in, pudgier than the first, with bleached hair and purple bangs. She'd razored off the sleeves of her sweatshirt. She sat down next to PJ Girl—er, Teresa—and nudged her with a box of tissues.

To Bones's right, another fat girl. To his left, a fatter girl. No way he'd survive six weeks of this.

"Welcome to the club, man," Lard muttered.

As the chairs filled up Bones realized little cliques had cemented long before he'd checked in—the shy and the loudmouths. He and Lard were the only guys. One, two, three...six females including a woman who looked to be in her early thirties. She wore a long strand of pearls and a sheer blouse with pleated slacks.

Bones figured she was a counselor. "She looks normal enough."

Lard opened his journal, jotted down something, and passed it to Bones. *Eve's a pediatric nurse.*

Dr. Chu appeared, clipboard in hand. He reminded Bones of the principal at his high school. They both had gray ponytails and trimmed soul patches. Dandruff sprinkled their dark shirts.

Dr. Chu stood behind Teresa, who was sniveling into a tissue. His hand rested lightly on her shoulder. "Don't be afraid to comfort someone in pain." His gaze moved from one downcast head to the next. "That's what we're all about in here. Helping each other through difficult times."

Dr. Chu had squeezed Bones's shoulder the same way during his orientation. He was like all the other therapists Bones had met over the years. Smug know-it-alls who didn't try to hide their smugness or know-it-all-ness.

"Does anyone have something to say to begin?" he asked.

Eve spoke up first. "Dinner last night was two ounces of boneless, skinless chicken breast. Doesn't anyone care about the pain of those chickens? Or the fuel squandered by the global production of chicken feed?"

Bones did a double take. Guess she wasn't a nurse working in the hospital, but a nurse in the program, as in a patient. "High-tech turnips..." she was saying. "Are we supposed to eat this stuff or is it going to eat us?"

Lard snorted under his breath. "Gotta love a woman with attitude."

"I insist on my right to substitute tofu for meat," Eve said.

*Smart*, Bones thought. Tofu is less than a third of the calories of the same amount of skinless chicken breast.

"I'll take it up with our nutritionist," Dr. Chu said, lost in the work of being a therapist. "I'd like everyone to welcome Jack Plumb."

"Hi, Jack," the room echoed.

Dr. Chu smiled with his mouth closed. "Everyone else, please introduce yourself."

"Elsie," said the girl with the bleached hair and razored sweatshirt. "Anyways, I entered the program as a chronic bulimic, but I haven't purged since I've been here."

"Bullshit," Lard muttered.

Eve introduced herself. "My medical records say I'm anorexic, but as you can see that's a misdiagnosis." She smiled, fingering her pearls. "People are just jealous of my figure."

Lard blushed.

God, Lard *liked* her.

Dr. Chu reached into his briefcase and pulled out a journal like Lard's. He handed it to Bones. "Every patient gets a journal."

"Thanks," Bones said.

"Anyone else have something they'd like to discuss?" Dr. Chu asked.

Bones counted imaginary red M&M's through a painfully long silence. The nurse gathered her pearls in one hand. She clearly considered herself better than the others. Her knowing smile said it all. The girl with purple bangs unraveled a thread from her sweatshirt. Lard stared out the window, as if calculating an escape.

Suddenly the girl in pj's burst into tears.

"Maybe it's time to talk about it, Teresa," Dr. said, without losing eye contact with the rest of the room.

Everyone held a collective breath waiting to see what would happen next.

"I-I-I can't...my mom..." Teresa sobbed into a tissue. "She'd kill me if she knew I said anything."

"It isn't healthy to keep things bottled up," Dr. Chu said. "You have to let it out."

"I just...don't think I can."

"Okay, Teresa. Whenever you're ready." Then Dr. Chu

announced that today's session was ending early and handed out a writing assignment. "Go back to your room, lie on your bed, and close your eyes," he said. "Picture an achievement in your life that made you feel proud and write about it."

# 4

Lard collapsed his folding chair and leaned it against the wall. Bones did the same and they headed back to their room. "Sounds like Eve lives here full-time," Bones said. "That doesn't inspire much confidence in the program."

"There's no magic pill for what we have," Lard said. "Especially if you don't admit there's a problem."

Bones found this type of amateur therapy annoying.

"Let's go to the kitchen and see what Gumbo's up to. Maybe he'll have a job for you that doesn't involve food. Last year I composted scraps, even started a vegetable garden on the roof."

"The hospital roof?"

"Chu Man doesn't know about it." Lard shrugged his burly shoulders. "I'd never be in one of those programs with locked doors and alarms. A guy can't go outside to fart if he has to."

"I hear you."

"Come on, I'll show you around the roof."

"Think I'll take a nap." Bones really just wanted to be alone for a while. The emotional dump in group therapy had worn him out. "Maybe work on my assignment."

"Okay, suit yourself."

Bones laid down on his bed and closed his eyes. He remembered the day his sister became editor of her school paper; the day his dad got a bonus for selling the most insurance policies; the day his mom hit the $10,000 mark for donations she'd raised for the food bank.

He opened his eyes and stared at the ceiling, thinking about the A he'd gotten on his mid-term paper and his parents whisking him and his sister off to a restaurant downtown. He'd slumped beneath a crystal chandelier, picking at his chicken piccata, pierced by guilt because he'd copied his essay from *Time* magazine and didn't have the balls to fess up.

..........

The next morning Bones woke up in a room too quiet for the amount of light pouring in through the window. He glanced at the clock on his desk: 6:45 a.m. Lard was noticeably absent, probably in the kitchen prepping breakfast.

Bones kicked off the starched sheets. He'd been awake most of the night worrying about his menus. Why hadn't they shown up yet? He laced his Converse, little one-pound weights on his feet, and ticked off ten minutes of jumping jacks. That burned seventy-five calories. Not enough. Never enough.

He went for another ten minutes. He struggled to catch his breath. Flashes of cold hit him. He shivered. His nose ran. Bones needed a scale bad, real bad. There was only one fix— sneaking into the examination room where the scales were kept. He remembered it being next door to the laundry room.

*That's it!* He'd act like he needed to do laundry. He studied Lard's dirty clothes heaped in the corner, sure Lard wouldn't mind if he washed them.

First he had to shower and change.

Someone knocked on the door even though it wasn't closed. "Anyone home?"

*Nancy, the nurse.*

"Yeah?" Bones hugged the wall by the closet, not wanting her to see him all sweaty like this. She'd know he'd been exercising.

"Are you decent?" she asked.

"I was about to hop in the shower."

"That sounds dangerous," she said, chuckling at her joke. "Just kidding. I'll slip your menus under the door."

"Thanks." Bones picked them up, staring at lunch. His throat closed up and his heart worked at recalibrating itself as he read the number of calories listed on the menu. Two-hundred-and-fifty: one-quarter-turkey sandwich on whole wheat bread with crust (125 calories), one-half medium apple with skin (40 calories), mixed green salad (40 calories) with one-tablespoon of balsamic vinaigrette (45 calories).

He knew his calories as well as he knew his ABCs.

Counting calories usually quieted his brain. But not today. Two-hundred-and-fifty calories were more than he'd consume all day at home. He'd have to jog three miles to burn it off—or find a way to exercise for half an hour by (1) swimming, (2) rock climbing, (3) or ice-skating. Not very likely in this place!

Bones showered and put on his XL sweats, because baggy made him look bulky, and maybe that would be enough to keep Dr. Chu from piling on more calories. He buffed his buzzed head. He'd first shaved it in middle school after reading about a mathematician who'd figured Rapunzel's fourteen-inch locks weighed fourteen ounces.

He'd once shaved his body too, even his eyebrows, which his friends said made him look like a hundred-year-old baby. He gave it up because the outgrowth drove him nuts.

Bones folded the menus and shoved them into his journal.

He had to find Dr. Chu.

Bones found his office down a long hall past the dayroom. He knocked and waited. Knocked again, waited some more.

*Where's the friggin' doctor?*

Cell phones and laptops weren't allowed in the program. Except for letters and occasional family therapy nights, any contact with the outside world was highly discouraged, according to the thick paperwork the hospital had had him and his parents sign.

Bones should have at least tried to smuggle his cell phone in so he could text his mom and tell her he was being poisoned or tortured or something. She'd realize the program was a mistake and come and take him home. He knew she would.

*Where is he?*

Bones didn't know he'd fallen asleep, sitting on the floor, until he heard Lard's voice. "You missed breakfast, man," he said. "You are so screwed."

# 5

Bones stared across a cluttered desk at a silent Dr. Chu who'd formed a steeple with his fingers while waiting to hear the reason for Bones's visit.

"Can I call my mom?" he asked, sliding lower in the fake leather chair.

Dr. Chu didn't answer. It was like he'd manipulated the second hand on his clock so it wouldn't move. Even the miniature ivy on his desk was dying under the strain of stopped time.

Finally Dr. Chu picked up the phone and dialed. "Nancy, please bring Mr. Plumb's breakfast to my office. He'll be dining with me this morning."

"But I've always been able to call home." Bones hated the desperate sound of his voice. "Anytime, any place."

"Sorry, Jack," he said. "Not from this place."

There was only one way to make it through this. "Can I...? I mean, is it okay...? Do you have...rubber gloves?"

Dr. Chu frowned over a drawer, pulling out checkers, jacks, cards, and a pair of latex gloves. "You may think I don't understand, but I do. Just give yourself time. It'll get easier."

Bones took the gloves, rolling them onto his fingers, exhausted all over again from the strain of the program. At least the calories from the impending feast wouldn't be absorbed through his fingers and stomach.

Nancy walked in holding the same type of cafeteria tray used at his high school. "Here you go, Jack." She smiled at him and left.

Bones stared at a cheap melamine plate with an omelet, fruit bowl, and dry toast.

"Is something wrong?" Dr. Chu asked.

*I have the stomach flu, sore throat, tooth abscess, migraine, allergy to gluten...I never eat breakfast on Wednesdays or in closed rooms or during a lunar eclipse, especially in July or when I'm out of deodorant...*

"I'm just not hungry."

"Take your time."

Bones cut the omelet in half, turned it, cut it in half again, and then once more. He couldn't breathe, dying the slow death of a bug on a fly strip. Fifty-three minutes and seventy-two bites later nothing was left on the plate except years of scratches.

· · · · · · · · · ·

Back in his room, Bones paced from the window to the door and back. He counted thirty twelve-by-twelve linoleum tiles, slapping the windowsill before turning around, petrified that fifteen minutes of speed walking wouldn't burn off breakfast.

Lard looked up from a celebrity chef cookbook. "You're driving me nuts!"

Bones hit the deck. First sit-ups, then he rolled over for push-ups. The tip of his nose grazed the towel he'd thrown on the floor. He blinked salt from his eyes, then felt a heavy weight on his butt, knocking the air out of him. "Get your skinny ass up," Lard said, releasing his boot. "I need a smoke."

Bones rolled out from under the boot. He had a really, really bad feeling about this. But he gathered up his sweaty self and draped the towel over his shoulder.

Lard pushed two cookbooks at him. "If anyone asks, you're helping me in the kitchen. Follow me."

"Okay."

Lard and Bones slowed at the dayroom when they saw Eve sitting on the couch sipping from a two-liter bottle of Crystal Light (5 calories per serving).

*Where'd she get that?*

Morning light filtered in, turning her wavy hair bronze. Her blouse was unbuttoned enough to show off the frilly lace of her bra. She'd kicked off her shoes, revealing perfect toes with cranberry polish.

Normally Bones didn't notice feet, but Eve was unbelievably *hot* for someone his aunt's age. *An experienced older woman*, he thought. When he felt himself harden under a thick blend of cotton and polyester he mentally did the times tables backward. Unfortunately it only worked part of the time.

Eve caught him staring. "How's your second day going?"

"You can call me Boner," he said like an idiot. "I mean *Bones*."

Lard snorted.

Eve smiled knowingly.

Bones tagged along behind Lard through the dayroom and down a corridor to a service elevator, trying to will his erection down.

"Nothing's going on until lunch," Lard said when the elevator opened. "So don't look so guilty."

Bones shrugged and followed him into the elevator.

# 6

The doors opened onto what looked like a storage area crammed with paint cans and rolls of carpet. Lard led the way to a fire door. Stenciled letters warned *restricted area. no exit: alarm.*

Lard bulldozed right through it. They emerged onto a portion of the roof about the size of a basketball court. A chain-link fence protected the perimeter, but the smoggy air smelled like freedom. "Come on."

They walked around a jumble of junk—antennas, air compressors, satellites—and rounded a corner to a smaller area with raised vegetable beds.

"I'll never buy food shot up with hormones when I own a restaurant," Lard said. "Chicken nuggets sound healthy enough, but they have more than three dozen ingredients—not a lot of chicken in a nugget."

Bones put on his gloves in case he'd have to touch something with calories, like dirt. "Can we talk about something else?"

"That's the wrong attitude, man. Don't you want to get over this shit?"

"Not at this particular moment, since it's almost lunch and my jaw still hurts from breakfast."

Lard shook his head. "I'm glad I don't live inside your skin."

"It'd be a little crowded." Bones was thinking this buddy thing was overrated. He gripped *Celebrity Chefs* in one hand, Rachael Ray in the other, and launched into bicep curls.

Lard probed the dirt with his fingers. "Peppers could use a drink," he said. "Get the watering can. Over there by the faucet."

Bones filled the two-gallon can and carried it back, pumping it up and down like a dumbbell. Lard squinted under his shag of hair. "One sick fuck."

"Aren't we all?"

"Some more than others, and some of us are just regular guys who wanna get laid." Lard dug at the base of a tomato plant. He unearthed a ziplock sandwich bag, kissed it, dirt and all, and dragged two chairs into the shade. "Have a seat."

The contents of the bag may have looked like dried oregano, but even a guy who'd led a pathetically sheltered life knew better than that. Lard took out a packet of Zig-Zags and brushed it off. He smoothed out the thin sheet of paper.

Bones watched while Lard pinched and sprinkled the dried stuff with precision. He licked a seam, rolled it easily, and twisted the ends.

"Are you crazy? Smoking that up here?"

Lard struck a match in reply. He lit up, inhaling. The tip glowed red. A seed popped, hitting his T-shirt, burning a tiny hole. So those weren't dots of Worcestershire sauce on his shirt after all. He held the joint out to Bones.

"That stuff's bad for your health," Bones said. "It gives you the *munchies*."

"Pot is one of your basic greens," Lard said, exhaling smoke. "It has all kinds of nutrients, even omega fatty acids. Pot, my friend, is part of the fucking food pyramid."

Lard snuffed the burning tip, put what was left in the bag, and offered up a mint. "Sugar-free."

. . . . . . . . . .

They worked their way back through the maze of junk—barely reaching the door when it flew open. A beanpole guy with mushroom cap ears emerged in chef clothes—white shirt with two rows of black buttons and the same type of pinstripe pants Lard wore. Suddenly he was in front of them, sniffing the air. Lard threw his arms around the guy like he'd been reunited with his long lost dad. "Gumbo!"

"Have you been smoking? I told you, if you get caught—"

"This is Bones," Lard said quickly. "In case you can't tell, he's anorexic."

"Pure?" Gumbo turned to study him. "Or purge?"

"Look at his teeth."

Bones smiled, offering proof in enamel.

"And no scars on his knuckles—I checked."

"Have they given you a job yet?" he asked Bones.

"Nuh-uh."

"I could use some help in the dayroom," Gumbo said. "Setting up tables and chairs for meals, then breaking them down afterward. I can talk to Dr. Chu if you're interested."

It sounded like calorie burning to Bones. "Sure, thanks."

. . . . . . . . . .

With little time left before lunch, Bones decided to work in his journal. He wished he could delete the memory of that fateful day in the department store with the insensitive sales clerk.

He flashed on the first time he'd worn his new *Huskies* to school. He'd been walking through the cafeteria when his plate of custard slipped off the tray. He'd knelt in the stiff knees to wipe up the mess when cross-eyed Valerie Willendorf shrieked, "Jack's eating off the floor!"

At first the room was quiet, in fact the space had never been so quiet, unless the principal was on duty. Then the kids fell all over each other laughing.

"Get the dork a fork!" Valerie again.

The rest of the year, anytime something spilled— watercolor in art class or slime during a science project— some jerk called out for Jack to lick it up. He'd heard, *Hey, Jack, suck it up* countless times. He only wished he'd had the guts to defend himself, gotten in their faces, and given it right back to them.

Bones went to the dayroom hoping the pain of homework would be lessened if Eve occupied the couch. He'd just sat down, disappointed not to see her, when Unibrow rounded the corner, pushing a wheelchair occupied by a slight girl, his jowls flushed under the strain.

The girl was connected to an IV line that ran from a clear bag on a pole clamped to the chair's back. She wore a low cut black leotard over thin black tights. Leg warmers ran from her ankles to the top of perfectly straight thighs. Her eyes were downcast, their color a mystery.

Bones tried to look away. But. Could. Not.

She was as thin as a hummingbird feather and just as translucent. So frail. So incredibly delicate. He drank in the sight.

The girl looked up and saw him staring. Her eyes were raw almonds, her freckles fine as sifted cinnamon.

Lard sauntered in, breaking the spell. "Hey there, Alice," he said. "I've been wondering when you'd show up. I'd ask how you've been, but that seems obvious."

She smiled in a way that commanded the room. "I've missed you too, you big tub of lard."

Just as suddenly, she was gone, wheeled down the hall. Bones stared at the space, swept away by perfection. He wondered where Unibrow was taking her. And when she'd be back.

# 7

The next two days passed in a blur of agonizing meals, painfully boring therapy sessions, and inane writing assignments. Bones couldn't shake the vision of Alice in the tight-fitting leotard and tights, like a thin layer of extra sexy skin. He sat alone in the dayroom with his journal, wondering if she'd been real.

The girl who'd been crying in therapy strolled in. Tamara? Tasha? No. Bones remembered her name was Teresa. Her makeup looked like it had been cried off. She wore a turquoise T-shirt, which she kept tugging over her voluminous butt.

Bones tried to think of something nice to say to make up for all the mean things he'd thought about her. Truth was he'd started judging fat people long before he'd started trying to lose weight. Twisted logic, for sure.

He tried to put himself in Teresa's place, imagining how hard it'd be to squeeze into the hospital's stall shower, how horrible it would be to see all that flabby flesh in the mirror.

But the images required her being naked so he shrugged them off.

Teresa picked up the TV remote and folded her overly stuffed self into an easy chair. She clashed with its sickly yellow and brown stripes. "Hardly anyone talks about shame," she suggested, noting his journal. "Or remorse. Dr. Chu would wet himself if you wrote about that."

Teresa surfed the channels, finally settling on a reality show about disgustingly fat people who were looking for someone to share their life with. "The guy on the left used to have a twin brother," she said. "But he ate him."

Bones laughed.

She smiled at him and he smiled back.

Teresa studied her reflection in the TV's dim screen, fiddling with the safety pin in her eyebrow. It looked dull.

She reminded Bones of a fat girl he met in a group therapy meeting a year ago. She'd been so depressed about her weight she'd quietly swallowed pills, chasing them down with Kaopectate to keep from throwing up. Her brother found her and called 911. Afterward she wore a hand-painted T-shirt to meetings to show she was learning to accept her body, *More to Love.*

..........

Bones set up folding chairs and tables for dinner before going back to his room, where he was horrified to see Lard eating cottage cheese (one-half cup, 90 calories) from the carton. Even the smell grossed him out.

"Sharing a room with another person is hard enough!" Bones rushed to open the window. "But a person bringing food into my personal space is not okay! And I'm lactose intolerant!"

"You can't be allergic to smells."

Bones heard the empty container hit the trashcan behind him. "Tell that to the twenty-three million people with hay fever."

"Trying to appear tragic in an eating disorder ward is redundant."

When Bones leaned out the window he saw a string of twine tied to a nail below the sill. A bag of Cheese Doodles (7 ounce bag, 975 calories, 99% fat) hung from a clip on the end. Definitely contraband.

"It could be worse, man," Lard said. "You could have a roommate who pukes in his pillow case. "Come on, it's time for dinner."

Bones felt shaky, unsteady at the thought of more food. The weight of regularly scheduled meals was so hard, and he hated other people deciding what he could and could not eat. The dayroom smelled like the burnt microwave burritos his sister bought at 7-Eleven. That and shattered hopes.

Lard pushed by him. "Let's sit with Eve."

To shake off impending doom, Bones noted that this was the first time he'd ever been invited to the popular table. Lard smoothed his hair self-consciously and chose a chair next to Eve. She wore shorts, an impressively tight

T-shirt, and the type of running shoes that caused serious wallet-cramping.

Bones sat across from her.

Teresa joined them. "Chu man gave me an extra ten minutes on the treadmill. What a killer."

That was the best news Bones had heard since checking in. "There's a gym in the hospital?"

"Physical therapy," Lard said. "But you won't start on a program until your weight's stable."

"That means he's going to force calories down you," Eve said with obvious disgust. "I could loan you a bra for weigh-in. Stuff it with something heavy so the scales show a gain. Then maybe he won't raise your calories so much."

"Why tell him that?" asked Teresa. "Look at him, he's thin as a toothpick."

"I am looking at him." Eve smiled. "He's perfect the way he is."

Lard leaned back dejected, as if everything he'd learned in life was dissolving before his eyes.

Bones sat there equally uncomfortable. There was nothing worse than having someone talk about you behind your back in front of your face. In the awkward silence that followed, Bones put on his gloves, letting the rubber snap his wrists. Eve looked at him sympathetically. "I feel your pain."

Another table filled up. Unibrow came in. His mustache bristled when he set down their trays, but he didn't say anything. He never did. Sometimes, if it weren't for his fingers gripping a mop handle or dinner trays, you wouldn't know he was alive.

Bones closed his eyes against the smell of decaying flesh on his plate—fear and despair for both the diner and the about-to-be dined. There wasn't enough oxygen in the room. He was dying inside, slipping into the outer edge of a bottomless chasm. Any rush about being at the "in" table had taken leave.

"They only gave you eight peas?" Lard eyed Bones's plate. "I could mainline those."

"It's not that I'm paranoid," Bones said, mashing the peas into his chicken. "But I'm pretty sure the peas have been talking about me behind my back."

Lard snorted.

Eve changed positions and two bumps strained against her T-shirt. She called Nancy over. "Can I have a saltshaker and some lemon wedges?"

Nancy came back with silverware, saltshakers, and lemon wedges.

Eve drenched her food in salt.

Bones did the same. It was the only thing that made food remotely palatable.

Then Eve squeezed lemon juice (1 calorie) into her water. "Lemon is a natural diuretic." She was so smooth, so smart.

Bones gagged down his dinner, then stormed the bathroom, flung off his clothes, and climbed on the overturned trashcan. He stared into the mirror, shrinking back. *Flab,* a vile four-letter word. Not part of the plan!

His strategy was to use the shower like a sauna, cranking the handle full-force to the left. His skin burned but it wasn't hot enough. Water should be boiling to melt fat. The stupid hospital probably controlled the thermostat.

Bones thought he heard his sister's voice, in the distance and fading fast. *I hope you get better in there.*

# 8

Lard stuck his head in the doorway. "Hang in there, man."
Bones slumped on the toilet lid, a towel tied around his waist.
"They're going to turn me into a raging Vomitus Interruptus,"
he said. "I love my white teeth!"

"No, man. You done good."

"Why don't I believe you!"

"No pain, no gain."

"I'll never make it another day," Bones said. "Not without
knowing exactly how many layers of fat I'm putting on."

Lard shook his head. "I give up."

Bones stayed in the bathroom until he was so cold he
had to get dressed.

Sometime after nine thirty he and Lard settled onto their
prospective concrete slabs of beds. Lard was into *Rachael
Ray 365: No Repeats: A Year of Deliciously Different Dinners.*
Bones flipped through a *Weight Watchers* article, "Weight
Loss Dos and Don'ts."

The biscuit from dinner felt like a depth charge in his stomach. "How long have you known Alice?" he asked.

"We hung out last summer," Lard said. "Her parents check her in, she puts on a few pounds, almost looks normal. I mean normal for her, but then she goes home and bakes laxative brownies. I love her like a sister, man, but I sure don't understand her."

"Does she have a boyf—" Bones couldn't get the word out.

"It figures you'd like her skinny ass." Lard snorted. "Better take a cold shower because you won't see her for a while. Not until she's stable enough to be taken off the IV. Then you'll see her plenty. She likes the roof."

"But does she—"

"I don't think she has a boyfriend, if that's what you're asking."

Bones let himself be overwhelmed by the kind of desire he'd only seen in movies and wondered if couples really did have sex while feeding each other Lean Cuisine— lying entwined afterward, making up poetry only they could understand. He wanted to stretch out beside Alice, count her freckles, play connect the dots with his tongue.

"...unless you count George," Lard said.

"George?"

"A guy we hung out with last summer."

"In the program?" Bones asked.

Lard nodded. "I still can't figure out how he smuggled

beer in here. But you don't have to worry about him. Alice was always making fun of his man boobs."

Bones dropped to the floor beside his bed, ignoring the dizziness in his sixth set of push-ups. He pictured Alice— the profile of her head and nose, the sexy curve of her neck. Just then Dr. Chu's leather loafers walked across the floor toward him.

"What have we here?" he asked in a tone that meant trouble.

"Bones is looking for a screw," Lard offered up quickly. "It fell out of the frame of my glasses."

"Here it is." Bones held up two pinched fingers and nothing else.

Dr. Chu acted like he bought it. "How're you doing?" he asked. "The first few days are the toughest."

From here, Dr. Chu's face looked too small for his head, like his creator had run out of clay. Bones wondered what Dr. Chu would say if he told him the truth. That he'd entered the program as a pristine specimen of anorexia nervosa—but was in immediate danger of becoming a person who throws up out the window.

"I'm okay," Bones said.

"People who vomit don't lose weight in the long run," Dr. Chu said, as if reading his mind. "Bodies adjust when they think they're being starved."

Lard slammed the cover of his cookbook. "Can't we talk about something else, like *ever?*"

Dr. Chu smiled again. He seemed to have a smile for every occasion, like a rack of greeting cards. "Gentlemen, lights out was ten minutes ago. Good night and sleep tight."

"Don't let the bedbugs bite," Bones said after he left.

"Yeah, man, they flippin' hurt when they bite." Lard got up and slapped off the light switch. Between the door being ajar and lights from the parking lot streaming in through the window, the room wasn't all that dark. Bones watched Lard's hulking mass move through the room.

Bones slipped under the covers tossing from one cramped position to another. The sheets were too stiff and too uncomfortable for his unstable state of mind. The mattress was hard as the floor. He felt like someone had stuck pushpins in his spine.

He finally got up and stumbled to the bathroom where he peed with taurine force. The color had lightened from Root Beer to Afternoon Lift, the herbal tea his mom drank when winding down after board meetings. Sure the last five days had been hell, but they had to have been hell for his family too. Bones knew no one at his house was sleeping.

Bones went back to bed. With the lights out the racket in the corridor seemed louder. He recognized Nancy's voice and a deep male voice. Then he heard a weird noise. EE—UUU—RRRR—ACK! It sounded like someone was throwing up. No, more like someone was knocking down a brick wall with vomit. "Lard? Did you hear that?"

Lard grumbled irritably. "What do you think?"

"Who do you think it is?"

"Who cares?"

Bones didn't really care, though he guessed it was Elsie. "What room will they put Alice in?"

"Her parents pay for a private room," Lard said. "The one next to us is empty."

Bones liked the sound of that.

"But that's just a guess, man."

"You'll think this is a little weird, but you know what I thought when I saw her? I imagined us in our very own tenth floor apartment. No elevator. Medicine balls instead of chairs. A futon, silk sheets."

"I can picture it, man. A living room furnished with weights, his and hers stationary bikes, a treadmill with a high-torque motor, electronic programming, and heart-rate monitor. *Jog to fitness in the comfort of your own home!*"

"And forget about a stove or refrigerator. We'll just have a wheelbarrow filled with my go-to M&M's. Digital scales strewn across the carpet, stepping stones of accomplishment."

Lard snorted. "Your bathroom will be stocked with over-the-counter laxatives. Liquids, tablets, wafers, gums, chocolate, herbal. Powders that dissolve instantly in water."

Bones laughed then turned serious. "Eve told me she's leaving."

"Yep."

"You don't sound very upset."

"I hope she never comes back," Lard said simply. "If that means she's getting better."

"It has to mean that, right? Otherwise why would she be going home?"

"She's over twenty-one, man," Lard said. "She can check out anytime she wants—"

"But she can never leave."

"Very funny."

Even though Bones had just met Eve, he knew he'd miss her.

Lard made a noise and Bones figured he was about to impart additional words of wisdom when the walls began to shake in a cacophony of snores. Bones sat up, felt under his pillow for his flashlight, and aimed the light on a blank page in his journal, thinking about his family and everything he'd put them through.

He saw himself in the hall when he first got here—watching himself as he dragged his duffel over the highly polished linoleum—watching his mom as she leaned unsteadily against the reception desk—seeing his cowardly self too chickenshit to look back for one last good-bye.

He was terrified to tell his family how *not* eating made him feel. How many hours he'd spent lying on his back with a ruler balanced on his hipbones. How he pictured a battalion of Pacmen marching inside his body, chomping away. How he'd awake to the sound of his stomach growling, ecstatic because it meant his body was eating itself.

If Bones's parents knew the whole disgusting truth about his relationship with his body, he'd be locked up longer than six weeks. And it'd be a different kind of hospital. Lard droned on, a head-splitting buzz saw. The entire hospital could barf its guts out in the ward and no one would hear them.

God, Bones needed a scale. *Bad.* He dropped to the floor and alternated crunches with push-ups. Within twenty minutes he was drowning in a pool of sweat. His body was doing what it did best—dissolving itself. The ultimate liquidation.

Then he crawled into bed and passed out.

· · · · · · · · · ·

The next day Bones rolled over in the too bright, too loud morning. He got dressed and sauntered down the too bright hallway. He was setting up a card table when he noticed a piece of paper taped to the table's underside. The lined paper appeared torn from someone's journal. The note itself was partially printed in pen and more hurriedly scribbled in smudged pencil, like it had been written at different times.

Bones undid the tape, careful not to rip the paper.

It was Calvin Webb who saved specie homo sapiens. All by strumming his guitar. No electric cords. No amplifiers. No distortion peddles. Just the sweet hum of calluses skimming steel strings.

He lost himself in solo rehearsals for a band

he'd heard about—a gang called CRAP (Criminally Rebelliously Adolescent Population), kids about his age rumored to have run away, setting up camp in some crumbling 20th century hospital. Supposedly, like him, they played illegal instruments ripped off from the state depository: assorted brass and drums, a piano with non-synthetic keys.

Calvin longed to join them.

Bones put the paper in his pocket, wondering who'd written it.

People wandered in slowly while Unibrow delivered breakfast trays. Bones wondered if Eve's absence meant she'd overslept. Or if she'd been discharged like she'd said. Then he wondered what part of the hospital Alice was in and wished he'd paid more attention to the map in the lobby.

Teresa and the new girl, another bulimic named Mary-Jane, mumbled while they ate, their heads down in conspiracy.

From what he could overhear, all of the guys they'd dated dumped them after finding out they threw up after said date had paid for a meal. Guess they were annoyed to find out their hard-earned dollars were being flushed down the toilet.

"Jerks," Teresa said.

Mary-Jane played with the fake braid clipped above her ear. "Assholes."

Lard didn't say much when he ate because he was really into his food. He actually liked it. Bones rolled on his gloves. He didn't say much either, partly because he never talked with food in his mouth, but mainly because he didn't want to do anything to make the ordeal last longer than necessary.

Bones gagged on the disgusting sounds of people chewing. The rest of his egg-soaked toast would fit in his pocket if Unibrow and a nurse he'd never seen before weren't circling the tables. He stared at his hands. His fingers were getting fatter. Another forty-three minutes and there wasn't anything left on his plate but half a grapefruit rind.

"I could've remained a wonderfully content anorexic with a future as an attic crawler," Bones said.

Lard looked confused.

"The guys who work in attics fixing insulation and stuff," Bones said, then joked, "or maybe I could've been a laxative salesman."

Lard smirked. "You'd soil your skivvies, man."

"That's why washing machines were invented," Mary-Jane added.

Bones wanted to die.

He needed a red M&M.

When most of the plates were empty, Unibrow and the nurse let down their guards, chatting in the corner. Bones took a chance and stashed two knives under his shirt, praying like hell no one in the kitchen counted utensils.

# 9

Most of the time, most of the girls wore pajamas to group session. Bones had to admit he liked it. Today, though, Teresa had on jeans that hung a little loose and a sweatshirt that read *Worries Go Better with Bagels*. She'd done something fluffy with her hair and had on lip gloss. She sat next to Lard, her thigh touching his. He seemed okay with it.

Bones thought of Alice and wondered if she always wore tights. They were so thin, almost like a delicate layer of skin. It suddenly seemed so simple he was surprised he hadn't thought of it before. Having a girlfriend who looked at the world the same way he did was just what he needed to improve his mood.

"Who finished their writing assignment about emotions?" Dr. Chu asked.

"Part of it," said Sarah, a girl who reminded Bones of a friend of his sister's because she also used her sunglasses like a headband.

"Sort of," said Nicole, a girl his age with braces.

"Anyways, I finished mine then went to get a snack," Elsie said, as obnoxious as ever. "And a mouse ate it. Then a cat ate the mouse. Like, *seriously*, I checked the litter box."

Everyone laughed.

Dr. Chu passed around rainbow markers. "Reread your assignment, then highlight every word or passage that expresses a feeling." He emphasized *feeling* with air quotes. "Literally or figuratively."

"What is this anyways?" Elsie asked. "Dumbbell English?"

"I don't mean to be disrespectful," Mary-Jane added. Her feet were on the rung of her chair, knees poking through intentionally ripped pj's. "But what's the point?"

Dr. Chu had a far-off look, like he was trying to come up with an intelligent answer. "Consider the word *sorrow*," he said. "It might mean a person is depressed or maybe heartbroken. Using general terms to describe a feeling can remove you from a more intimate experience of said emotion. So whenever possible, try to be specific."

It was hard to listen to someone who continually talked out of his ass. Especially someone with gravy stains on his tie.

"Who'd like to share?"

Lard frowned, took off his glasses, rubbed his nose.

Bones picked lint off his sweats. Teresa bent forward like she might have something to say then changed her mind and leaned back.

Sarah chewed on the tip of her sunglasses. "I used to go to the market and fill my cart with food I wasn't going to buy," she said, speaking up. "I'd walk up and down the aisle eating about a million doughnuts then stash the empty boxes."

Bones listened, even though he'd heard plenty of stories like hers. "I scarfed down all that food without tasting it—without really seeing it. I don't know how to explain it…"

Sarah positioned her glasses back on her head and glanced at Dr. Chu. He nodded for her to go on.

"It was like some twisted high," she said. "Stashing the empty boxes was the same as pretending the doughnuts had never existed. Like I never ate them in the first place."

This realization made Bones more sympathetic to her particular illness, even though, technically, she'd been shoplifting, not that he cared.

Most people thought anorexics didn't eat at all. *We eat too!* he wanted to shout. *Just not the same as the rest of you. Standing at the kitchen scraping macaroni from the pot because standing-up-eating calories count less than sitting-at-the-table calories. Stealing a bite of chocolate cake off his sister's plate because those calories count less than when they're on your own plate.*

He thought about his sister's birthday party a couple of years ago when her friends came over for cheesecake. He'd only taken a bite before shoving his plate aside. "I'd pay a million dollars for your self-control," Amanda had said. She'd been Jill's best friend since kindergarten. Before that, she'd hardly said two words to him.

"I'd trade my SAT scores to be skinny," another friend jumped in. "I just don't have any will power when it comes to dessert."

"Highest bidder wins," Bones said, soaking up the attention.

Amanda had squeezed his arm affectionately, as if pinching off bits of will power. It made him feel important, because he had something she wanted. That had never happened to him before.

After that he began eliminating certain things from his diet. Not all at once, but slowly. Within a couple of months he was living on grapefruit, low-fat yogurt, and M&M's. That kind of self-control was intoxicating. Just another couple of pounds, he kept telling himself. Then another couple to make sure he had a cushion.

Bones weighed himself constantly, thrilled as the numbers dipped below normal. He was making his own rules and it felt great. Pretty soon girls at his school began to notice. "Have you seen Jack?" he heard them whisper in the halls. "How do you think he did it?"

Bones had never felt such power.

He was happily addicted.

Sarah was still talking. "I'd be so depressed I'd sit in my car and throw up in a plastic bucket." Then she started talking super fast, like she had to get it all out or die. "I'd tell myself it was the last time, but—"

Elsie nodded, like she got it. "The only way to be noticed in this town is to be skinny."

"It's hard not to buy into that crap when everything in our society is either black or white," Nicole said. "Good or bad. Fat or thin."

"We have to find middle ground," Mary-Jane said. "And stop obsessing about our screw-ups."

Teresa hugged her knees. She was staring out the window at something that wasn't there. "I know why I'm fat," she said quietly. "And I think I understand why I turned to food to—" She choked herself off.

Bones glanced at her sideways.

"I, uh, I didn't want guys to like me. I didn't want anyone to touch me again. *Ever*. Like that dirtbag who used to live next door. I babysat his kids…and this one night he came home early without his wife.

"I was on the couch watching a rerun of a dumb show about models. He stood behind me, which was creepy enough. Then he started rubbing my neck, asking me about school and stuff. I was terrified…"

Teresa wiped her nose on her sleeve.

Nicole passed her a tissue.

Everyone waited.

The air was being sucked from the room.

"Afterward, I ran home and told my mom."

Lard reached for her hand but she pulled it away.

"She rocked me and whispered, *Hush, Angelita, hush.*" Teresa took another tissue, trying not to let her voice shake. "The next morning Mom wouldn't look at me, like she was suddenly ashamed of me or something. She made me promise not to tell anyone..." She dropped her head into her hands. "He took something away from me, and my mom let him do it."

"Fucking creep," Elsie said. "And your mom—I can't believe she treated you like that."

Bones wished he could say something to help. This wasn't the first time he realized he'd spent too much time alone with his own thoughts, overanalyzing things to the point that he couldn't think or act like a normal person. His shoulders rose and fell. He tried to look—what? Sympathetic? Yeah, that was it.

Nicole shook her head and shrugged. "*God.*"

Lard took off his glasses to rub his eyes.

Teresa let her hands fall into her lap. "That's when I started pushing people away. Guess it worked because my friends stopped calling—not because I'd gotten fat—but because I spent every afternoon in front of the TV eating ice cream from the carton with a soup spoon.

"When I got tired of being alone it was too late. All those years gorging on take-out in the middle of the night...I was stuck in this crazy cycle of using food to make me feel better," she said quietly. "Guess I was a victim—a victim of myself."

Dr. Chu got up when Teresa looked like she was going to dissolve into herself. "You're a survivor," he said gently. "Not a victim."

Teresa wiped snot and tears with the back of her hand. "On my last birthday I decided I wasn't going to let that asshole control my life. So I wrote him a letter, tore it up, dropped it in the toilet, and peed on it."

Bones thought she was the bravest person he'd ever met.

# 10

Something must have happened because the next day Lard blew his top. He kicked over the wastebasket, sending an empty cracker box across the floor. "You know what I said about my mom? She wasn't in a commune. That was pure unadulterated bullshit. She's a second grade teacher at Northridge Elementary School. You want to know the truth about my dad?"

Bones closed his magazine. "I guess. What's up?"

"I've been thinking about Teresa, man. You know, what she went through." His nose dripped and his glasses steamed up. "She had the guts to tell the truth about what happened to her, so I thought I'd tell someone about my dad. Unless you're too fucking busy."

"Go ahead."

Lard's fists were two boxing gloves. "He's number 87305. Cellblock 11. Folsom State Prison. A shit-for-brains loser who forges checks because he thinks he's too good for a regular job."

Bones said the only thing he could think of. "Want to hit the roof?"

"Oh, crap. We're supposed to go on an outing, like five minutes ago."

"Where?"

"Who knows?"

The so-called outing turned out to be a fifteen-minute walk to the drugstore to buy toothpaste, deodorant, and other necessities. It was one of those postcard days—the sky clear and the temperature in the upper-seventies—and it felt good to get away from the hospital.

Bones was surprised Dr. Chu had given him permission to go with the others, especially since he wasn't allowed to exercise. The thought of his impending first official weigh-in hung over him like a large, looming shadow in the fires of anorexic hell.

When they got to the store, Bones made an excuse for not going inside. "Forgot my wallet," he said.

The truth was Bones didn't trust himself to be around diet pills, diuretics, and laxatives, knowing he could probably hide them in his shoes or socks.

Bones found a bench and caught sight of his distorted reflection in the window. He stared into the glass, reenacting his wildest fantasies about Alice, until Nancy walked into the picture, staking out the cash register, a benevolent yet formidable guard. Three was definitely a crowd.

Lard and Teresa strolled out carrying small bags. "I picked up the new *Weight Watchers*," Lard said.

Bones got up from the bench. "Thanks, I'll pay you back."

"No need, my man."

. . . . . . . . . .

Back in the ward, Bones, Lard, and Teresa set up the Scrabble board. Still no Alice. Bones was looking for a place to play C-O-V-E-T when he heard the familiar rub of Nancy's pantyhose. She gave Bones an envelope. "Something from home," she said. "Your sister dropped it off."

"Thanks." He thought the no-personal-visit rule during the first month was ridiculous.

"Sorry, guys." He scooted his chair back and headed to his room, ripping open the envelope. The stationery smelled like his sister. Vanilla. He sat on his bed, relishing every word:

Hey there, little brother. Miss us? Mom has been more compulsive than ever since you left. As if heading two nonprofits isn't enough, she started volunteering at the library, which means there's never time for us to just sit down and talk. Only one of a million reasons why I miss you! She's been checking out books about eating disorders. Guess we're all trying to understand what happened to our favorite guy and what we can do to help him. Dad's been his crazy workaholic self so I'm feeling more like an orphan than ever. I know you've only been gone six days, but I miss not having anyone to torture. Write back soon, okay? Love you tons!

Your big sis, Jill.

P.S. Can't wait to see you on Family Night!

When Bones shoved the letter in a bottom drawer of his desk, he noticed a wad of paper. He smoothed it out on his desk:

Calvin hunkered over his rusty handlebars, pedaling his ten-speed above the transit tube that linked one underground metropolis to the next. Up here in the screwed-up ozone, all was as quiet as the day personal responsibility became illegal.

He sweated inside his black wetsuit, black skullcap, black combat boots, hoping all this blackness would help him blend into the inky night.

Another curfew violation and he'd get a permanent ankle monitor—an umbilical cord of the invisible kind, making sure His Excellence knew his whereabouts 24/7, as if he and everyone weren't spied on constantly as it was.

Calvin rode back to his zone, a dark figure among rats with gray, expressionless faces. North America had the biggest rodent population in the world, all those subterranean sewers.

He held fast to his handlebars and the belief that there were others like him who resisted the state's insipid laws; others who risked punishment to express themselves in any way they chose; others who thought that what a person dreamt was more important than endless essays that tested how little a person remembered about his past.

Other times he wasn't so sure. If only there was evidence beyond whispers during blackouts. He wondered if the world's enemy was real or imagined. Who knew in a society where lies were truth and truth was unknown?

Bones remembered the other part of the story. He wasn't sure where this piece fit in—but he was intrigued by Calvin and his collapsing world—and wondered if more of the story was stashed on the ward. He went to his closet, searched his pockets, and fastened the two installments together.

He was putting the pages in his drawer when he noticed Lard had left his lunchbox behind. *What's in that thing anyway?* He was about to take a peek when Lard startled him from behind. Bones knew he was busted.

"Don't even think about it, man."

"What?"

Lard grabbed his lunchbox. "Meeting in five minutes."

Bones and Lard strolled in late but not by much. Bones wondered which one of the girls would harass them about it. Thankfully they all seemed to be in their own self-absorbed orbits. Elsie looked like a solid block of granite in a skirt that was too short and too tight. There was tight but this was ridiculously tight.

The dayroom smelled like clothes left in a washing machine too long. Bones sat in a clammy sweat, worrying like he always did before a group meeting. "Anyone have a needle and thread?" he asked. "I have a hole in my pocket."

"Use the stapler," Sarah said from the couch.

"Crazy glue." Nicole this time.

Dr. Chu came in wearing his death and annihilation expression. His gaze rolled over the room to make sure no one was missing. Today's shirt had what looked like a mustard stain. "Can someone name a component that plays a part in eating disorders?"

Bones thought about warped reflections in storefront windows and car hoods.

"Personal weirdness," Nicole muttered under her breath.

"Sometimes I don't feel like I'm good enough?" Teresa said it like a question.

Dr. Chu opened his notebook. "Inadequate?" he asked her.

"Yeah, especially around people I don't know. I guess that's the same as low self-esteem."

Dr. Chu acted like he'd never heard it before. "What are some of the interpersonal factors that contribute to these issues?"

"Loneliness," Elsie said predictably. "Anyways, I'm *not* lonely."

Bones wanted to shout, *What about love, death, myths, religion, school, and deviant websites because life itself is what screws people up?*

The discussion droned on and on until Dr. Chu gave them an assignment. "I want you to write twenty-five sentences that begin *I'm grateful for...*" As if that wasn't bad enough he said they had to stand in front of a mirror and smile at themselves for a full minute. Like, they're supposed to be extra proud for having all their teeth?

After the meeting Lard and Bones zombie-walked down the hall to their room, where Lard hunkered at his desk eating Cheese Doodles from the bag that had been hanging outside the window. "These don't have as much polyunsaturated fat as most junk food," he said, squinting at the label. "In case you ever feel the urge to indulge."

Bones tried to ignore the fumes. "How'd you sneak those in here anyway?"

Lard crushed the empty bag and slam-dunked the wastebasket. "I could tell you but I'd have to kill you."

"Yoo-hoo?" Nancy peeked in, holding up a spool of thread. "Do you still need a needle and thread?"

"Yeah, thanks," Bones said. "Do I have to sign for it or anything?"

Nancy set the spool on his desk. "Just return it when you're done."

Bones waited for her to leave before pulling a stolen

hospital gown from his pillowcase. One size fits none. He ripped out the hem then went to the bathroom for the plastic bag he'd hidden in the tank behind the toilet. Inside were the two butter knives he'd stolen from the dining room, ready for their new purpose.

Bones sat on his bed, threading the needle. He positioned each knife over the ripped hem.

"I don't get it," Lard said. "Don't you wanna know how much you weigh?"

"Yeah, just not how much I've gained. And what's up with the old-school scales?"

"The hospital is too cheap to go digital."

When Bones first got to EDU all he could think about were the scales. But after gorging himself three times a day for six days straight, the thought of a weigh-in terrified him.

"I want Dr. Chu to think I put on more weight than I have," he said.

"You don't eat enough to keep a gnat's fart alive," Lard told him. "I don't know where you get the energy to exercise like you do."

Bones folded the hem over a knife and sewed it in place. "If Dr. Chu thinks I'm gaining weight he won't tack on any more calories. Right?"

Lard shrugged his beefy shoulders. "I know you don't believe me, man, but if you balance the calories you take in with those you burn off you won't gain weight. Like I said—"

"It's science." They said in unison and cracked up.

Then Bones rolled up the gown, shoved it in his pillowcase, and obsessed about a late night bed search.

· · · · · · · · · ·

Bones was alone in the dining room, arranging tables and chairs so everyone could have at least a small view out the pathetic window. From somewhere down the hall an old song blared from a radio, "We've only just begun…"

And there she was again, Alice, wheeling herself into the room. She'd tied a sheer skirt over her leotard. Her nipples pressed against the tight material. The IV line was gone.

"This place isn't exactly no-boys-allowed," she said, cracking her gum. Sugarless gum kept gastric juices flowing when the stomach had nothing to digest. "There's Lard, of course. You're his roommate, right?"

"Yeah." He tried not to stare, thinking how little she wore—just three thin garments—and how easily he could slip a finger under the strap of her leotard. He'd thought about sex before, plenty of times, but until now he'd never fully understood the concept of *making love.*

"You're the first male anorexic I've seen in here." Alice maneuvered her wheelchair around tables and chairs, moving so close Bones could smell Bubblicious.

"This stupid chair doesn't mean anything," she said. "A hospital rule so my parents can't sue, since I was in ICU for ventricular tachycardia."

Bones wasn't sure what that meant. "Sounds serious."

"My heart races sometimes. No biggie. I was only in

there three days this time, doesn't that prove it?" she said, smiling up at him. "Do you want to hear my theory?"

He nodded.

"There are two types of parents. Those who will do anything for their kids and those who will pay someone else to do anything for them. My parents are the second type—real control freaks, believe me—just like the Chu Man."

Bones laughed. "Dr. Dictator."

"He's a narcissist egomaniac," she said, fragile as an eggshell. "He gets off on having people depend on him."

Bones had to agree.

"He only wishes he had my discipline. And you should see the staff fridge. Non-dairy creamer, fat-free yogurt, diet sodas, rice cakes. I've seen Bruno make craft projects with fruit roll-ups."

"Really?"

"Have you always been so gullible?"

"Only on Tuesdays. And right before dinner."

Alice laughed, her delicate shoulders rising and falling. "The longer Chu Man keeps us dependent on him, the longer we end up staying here and the more money he makes."

Bones hadn't thought of it that way.

"If you don't cooperate you're transferred to a higher care facility," she said. "Which is no fun, believe me, with even more rules and a higher number of staff-to-patient ratio."

"You've been in a program like that?" he asked.

"You can't get away with smoking in those places," she

said, ignoring his question and cracking her gum. "Has Lard taken you to the roof?"

Bones was about to answer when Nicole and Sarah barged into the room, breaking the spell with their idiotic chatter. They commandeered a table like it was their last supper. Even Alice seemed annoyed by the interruption.

"I hope they get liver and onions for dinner," she said.

# 11

The arms of Alice's wheelchair fit snuggly under the card table, giving her a view beyond the parking structure. Bones sat across from her thinking how beautiful she was in her quietness, as if she knew something the rest of the universe didn't.

Elsie eyed Alice in the wheelchair and strolled over to introduce herself. "Anyways, food isn't the issue."

Alice just smiled.

Teresa stopped by next. "I had a breakthrough this week," she said, trying to sound encouraging.

Alice smiled again.

When she smiled like that her teeth were as dazzling as her tiny diamond earrings. She was anorexia nervosa in the purest form. Bones was impressed and inspired—knowing it was possible to go through the program without giving in completely to the radical beliefs of the EDU. Simply put, Alice hadn't let them brainwash her.

Nancy broke the spell. "Alice! I was afraid I'd never see you again."

"You know better than that," Alice said.

"Actually I was *hoping* I'd never see you again." Nancy took Alice's wrist in her hand, checking her pulse. "I've been doing some research into"—she paused, glancing at the others—"into cases like yours."

"Don't I always bounce back? Stronger than ever?" Alice said. "Come on, admit it. You know I do."

Nancy wore the expression of an overprotective parent. She jotted Alice's blood pressure onto a spiral pad. "We'll talk later," she said. "Right now, I have to help with the dinner trays."

"I didn't know you'd been here before," Teresa said. "Bet I sounded like a real know-it-all."

"Not at all," Alice said emphatically.

Bones slipped on his gloves, hoping Alice wouldn't think he was some psycho-serial-strangler and immediately realized that he'd never be able to feel her skin through his gloves.

He played lamely with the pepper shaker as Nancy set down Teresa's tray then watched, astounded, while Teresa dumped an entire packet of grated Parmesan cheese over her angel hair pasta (200 calories or 38 minutes on a stationary bike). The pasta was already loaded with diced tomatoes, zucchini, and onions (50 calories or one and a half miles speed-walking).

Alice had to look away.

"Parmesan is only twenty-two calories per tablespoon," Teresa said, as if she knew what they were thinking. "I burn that much watching TV."

Then Nancy set down Alice's tray. "Gumbo cooked your vegetables the way you like them," she said. "Steamed, no oil."

"Thanks." Alice plucked a white envelope from her tray. "What's this?"

"A note from Lard."

Alice used her knife to slit the flap. "*Welcome back!*" she said, reading. "*Now go home. Love, Lard.*" She looked up beaming. "God, I love that guy!"

Bones tasted the word *love*, a combination of Tabasco and Splenda. Fiery and sweet. He held it in his mouth, forbidden calories.

Alice's dinner consisted of one-half cup medium-grain white rice (120 calories), four spears of asparagus (20 calories), and a pat of butter (40 calories). Bones watched as she used her index finger to smear the butter on an asparagus spear. Then she sucked her middle finger, pretending to remove the excess butter. The buttered finger scratched an ankle, and the calories disappeared into a leg warmer.

"Tricky," he said under his breath.

She smiled conspiratorially. "Just good technique."

Nancy set down Bones's tray next.

Alice studied his pat of butter like a logic puzzle that needed solving. "Ask Nancy for a cup of hot water and a chicken bullion cube," she whispered to him. "Tell her your carrots don't have any flavor."

Bones did what she said; Nancy obliged.

Alice told Bones to stir the cube into the hot water until it dissolved. "Now pour it over your butter and carrots," she said. "Only eat the carrots."

"But—?"

"Trust me."

He choked down the disgusting orange roots (27 calories).

"It's okay to leave the bullion on your plate," Alice said. "Because it wasn't on your menu."

Bones figured it out. He'd get away with leaving the melted butter too.

. . . . . . . . . .

Later that evening, Bones and Lard were in Alice's room helping her put up a poster. Bones looked around trying not to look like he was looking around. He'd never been in a girl's room before (except his sister's). It looked bigger than his and Lard's because there was only one bed.

Newspaper clippings cluttered her bulletin board: auditions with ballet companies in Los Angeles, San Francisco, New York. Ballet shoes were lined up on her dresser—their ribbons hanging over the edge. A poster with a guy in white tights was unrolled on her bed.

"Nureyev," she said, noticing him noticing. "In his famous role as Romeo."

Lard knelt on the bed holding the poster flat against the wall. One hand was on the guy's package. "Is it straight?" Lard asked.

"Are you?" Alice deadpanned.

"Eat me," he said.

They busted up.

Bones pressed tape over the poster's corners. "How do dancers stand on their toes anyway?"

When Alice took a shoe from her dresser her skirt did that sexy flutter thing. "The toes aren't made of wood like most people think," she said. "It's layers of cardboard and glue, like papier-mâché. Here, feel it."

Bones took her shoe, breathing in the savory smell of her sweat.

"Did you bring me anything?" Lard asked.

"Hidden inside my yoga mat," she said. "With my smokes."

"Anybody home?" It was Nancy.

"Just us psychos," Alice called back.

Nancy came in only mildly surprised to see Bones and Lard. "No guys allowed in your room after 8 p.m.," she told them. "There I said it, just for the record. So where's your wheelchair?"

"Fuck the chair," Alice said.

Nancy suppressed a smile.

··········

Bones woke to a beefy fist shaking him. His bedspread was

pulled up tight around his neck and he was clutching his pillow to his chest. Microfiber armor. He didn't know what time it was, but a drab light streamed in through the curtains.

"Wake up, man," Lard said. "It's time to get weighed."

"Huh?"

Lard chuckled. "No, man, I said *weighed.*"

Bones propped himself on an elbow, glancing at the clock. Seven forty-three. Weigh-in was scheduled for eight. He'd slept in sweats, like always, and smelled like the inside of a neglected gym locker.

"Should I change in here?" he asked. "Or the laundry room?"

"In there." Lard threw his bedspread haphazardly over his bed. "Don't worry, it'll be over in a flash."

Bones rushed through his bathroom routine. His pee smelled like cat piss. He flushed. He used his towel to clear a swath in the foggy mirror. And there he was, all bloat and jowls.

Lard's voice came through the open door. "Don't sweat it, man."

"People only say that when there's something serious to worry about," Bones shot back.

"Just trying to help."

Bones rummaged through his closet for clean sweats, changed, and grabbed his gown. "Yeah…okay…sorry," he said, rushing out, as the knives faced off in the hem of the gown.

The door to the examination room opened just as he got there. Teresa came out still in her gown. No bra, he noticed, looking away.

"I lost seven more pounds," she said. "It feels good, you know, not to be puking in a gas station bathroom after binging on hamburgers. Even the sores in my mouth have healed. Sorry, I didn't mean to..." Her voice dropped to a whisper. "I know you think that stuff's gross."

Bones raised his shoulders. "It's okay."

"It's so not okay, Bones. I don't ever want to be that person again." She shook her head in that way of disbelief. "I never thought I'd be able to eat like a normal person and lose weight."

"You're up next," Unibrow said from the doorway.

..........

Bones sat hunched in the droning silence of the too-bright office. The overhead light sounded like it was full of dying flies. Dr. Chu's fingers were never still, unless they were forming a steeple, and even then they *tap, tap, tapped*. Bones wanted to break them off. *Snap, snap, snap.*

Bones knew what was about to happen.

Dr. Chu confirmed it. "How are you feeling today?"

It was a trick question.

Bones let his eyes roll back in his head, trying to figure out what Dr. Chu wanted him to say. The truth was, he felt like crap. Unibrow had noticed the sagging hem in his gown when Bones stepped off the scales. Unibrow didn't seem surprised. More like, *Knives? Not very original.*

"Can you tell me why you added weight to your gown?" Dr. Chu asked.

Another trick question.

Bones shrugged. "I wanted you to think I was gaining weight."

Dr. Chu nodded. "We need accurate records for every patient."

*(Our job is to make sure you gain as much weight as possible while you're here.)*

Dr. Chu leafed through Bones's file, checking off little boxes. "Since you lost weight—even with two stainless steel knives in your gown, it's obvious you've been purging. Either by vomiting or—"

*(We have closed-circuit cameras and hidden microphones in your room.)*

"Or engaging in unauthorized exercise."

*(Bingo!)*

"I know this may be difficult," Dr. Chu said. "But the nutritionist and I have decided to raise your calories."

*(We won't be satisfied until you resemble a scrap-fed hog.)*

"Are you listening to me, son?"

Bones's eyeballs hurt from so much nodding. "Yes, sir."

*(Fuck you!)*

"One-hundred calories isn't as bad as it sounds." Dr. Chu dropped his voice, forcing Bones to lean forward in his chair. "That's it for now."

Bones got up and headed to his bathroom, where he stripped, cold and shaking. He stood on the overturned waste can, knowing he'd never see his ribs again. Not with an extra one-hundred calories per day. He focused on his collarbone, his sternum. His reflection flashed: *The object in mirror is larger than it appears.*

He grabbed the can of shaving cream and doused his pathetic self in menthol foam.

# 12

Lard sat slouched at his desk reading *Great Meals for Couples or Crowds.* He'd added two-for-one restaurant coupons to his bulletin board. "How'd it go with Chu Man?" he asked, looking up.

"I feel like I've sucked a dozen raw eggs," Bones said.

"Don't do that, man." A Lard snort kicked in. "You'll get salmonella."

Bones passed the rest of the afternoon in an invisible cloud.

The only thing clear was Alice's absence. Nancy said she was downstairs undergoing tests and took the opportunity to explain the seriousness of electrolyte imbalance. *Blah, blah, blah.*

Bones opened his journal and flipped to his last entry. He'd been writing about the day the scales dipped below 107 lbs. *I felt like I'd sunk the winning basket in a tie-breaker game because that's how people treated me. Being skinny made me a winner.*

He closed his journal, barely remembering he'd written that. He and Lard decided to spend the hour before dinner on the roof. Bones was surprised to see Alice there, lounging on a yoga mat.

"Hey there," she said, smiling at him.

Bones shook off his cloud of doom and stepped into a world of sunshine. "Hi."

He blinked at the pale skin peeking through her ripped tights, then noticed cotton taped inside her elbow. "Damn vampires," he said.

She tucked a strand of strawberry behind her ear. "And I still have to down an eight ounce glass of some sodium crap."

"That doesn't sound good," Lard said.

"You have an amazing power for stating the obvious," she said and shrugged. "I suppose they'll want a sample of my scales to see if I'm a fish."

Bones laughed.

But Lard said, "You'd better get back before they come looking for you."

"You used to be more fun," she said. "Besides, the lab's a certified zoo—they won't miss me for days." Then she asked Bones to help untie her yoga mat. "The string has a knot."

He bent down beside her, blinded by suntan oil glistening on her chest. Apparently she'd cut a hole in the mat's seam because she slipped her hand easily inside. She made a face in concentration and drew out a silver case, matches, and a foil packet.

"There you are, you little beauties." She tossed the packet to Lard. "Turkey jerky," she said. "Low fat. No MSG, artificial coloring, or flavorings."

"And I have something for you," he said, handing her a tube of hemorrhoid cream.

"Awesomeness!" Then she explained to Bones, "I rub it on my feet to numb the pain. Pointe shoes can be a real killer."

Who knew hemorrhoid cream was multitalented?

Alice sat on the mat with a cigarette between her delicious lips.

"Sorry, I have to ration them," she said, lighting up. Even though everyone knew smoking could kill, she looked amazing doing it. "I don't know how long I'll be stuck here this time."

"I don't smoke," Bones said.

She tilted her head. The sun peeked over the edge of the roof, turning her arm hairs bronze. Bones wanted to lick them, calories be damned. "Not anything?" she asked.

"Nope."

"Cigarettes curb your appetite, unlike—" She paused watching a white ribbon of smoke curl up.

As if on cue Lard lit a joint.

Alice spread her legs into a perfect V. Her muscles were long and taut. She stretched over one leg and then the other. Bones almost passed out when she stretched forward between those same widely spread legs. He wanted to kiss all her stretchiness right then and there and everywhere.

"I have an audition in a couple of weeks with a new ballet company," she said, sitting up. "It's at the opera house downtown. You should see it. Amazing, with crystal chandeliers and velvet seats."

Bones remembered the bus ride to and from the theater more than the theater itself. "Our class went there in fourth grade," he said. "There was a car lot down the street with a Felix the Cat sign."

"That cat's famous, man," Lard said, dragging a chair over. "Historical."

Alice tapped ash into a paper cup. "Did you see the dressing rooms? I practically grew up in them. My parents are actors. Sometimes they direct."

"Cool," Bones said.

Alice snuffed her cigarette. "Not really."

Lard inhaled, coughing. "Will you be able to dance that soon?"

Bones was wondering the same thing.

Alice ignored him. "A real friend would help me find a place to practice my leaps."

"What about up here?" Bones suggested.

"Too rough on my shoes." She stood up and made her way across the roof, clutching her tube of cream.

Bones watched her go.

Lard took another hit. "I hate to say it, but she'll never change."

"Who wants her to?"

"I mean, change, as in, get better. She's in and out of here so often they could name a revolving door after her."

Lard might have known her longer, but that didn't mean he knew her better. "I can help her," Bones said.

"Isn't that like the blind leading the blind?"

"Says he who resorts to Biblical idioms."

Lard chuckled and smoke seeped through his nose. "She's my friend and I'm fiercely loyal, you know that. But you have to admit it, man, she doesn't even have boobs."

"Sure, she does. They're just not as big as yours."

Lard snort-laughed. "Well played."

..........

Bones woke up sometime after midnight stressing out all over again about his weigh-in. No way he could have dropped to ninety-nine pounds. Not with all the calories they were forcing down him. It didn't make sense.

He stared at the ceiling, picturing Lard and Teresa hunched over their plates, shoveling in endless calories. Yet they said they were losing weight too. He wondered how much the scales were off? One pound? Three? Ten? Unibrow must have switched scales before Bones came in yesterday.

A loud clang in the corridor, then one word made it into the room. *"Shit!"*

Bones wondered if it was a patient sneaking around in

the hospital, then decided it was probably an exasperated nurse going out for a smoke. He worried himself back to sleep; he'd had a lot of practice at that.

··········

Alice wasn't at breakfast, which gave him more to worry about. He sat with Lard and Teresa and tried to figure out how to get rid of his corn flakes. (1 cup, 100 calories. Half cup low-fat milk, 60 calories. One bruised banana, 100 calories.)

"There's something going on with the scales," Bones said.

Lard sopped up two runny egg yolks (110 calories) with what was left of his whole-wheat toast (128 calories). He stuffed the entire disgusting wad in his mouth. "Let me guess. You lost weight so Chu Man raised your calories?"

"That's what I thought when I lost a pant size," Teresa said. "But it isn't the scales."

"Waistbands don't lie," Lard added.

Bones had stopped listening. He was keeping an eye on Nancy, who was standing watch over the room. She winced, apparently from a pantyhose wound—nail polish patched the run.

Today Mary-Jane's clip-on braid was blue. "Can I have a warm-up on my tea?"

Bones shoved his banana into his pocket when Nancy picked up the pot of hot water. When she filled Mary-Jane's cup, he untied his tennis shoe and sat it on his lap. *Two seconds.* That's all he needed to get rid of the rest of his milk and cereal.

82

Then, as if things weren't bad enough, Dr. Chu walked in and looked around like he was about to interrupt himself. "Sexuality Group will be at ten o'clock instead of eleven." He straightened his smiley face tie and left.

"No need for Bones to attend the sex meeting," Mary-Jane said.

Elsie smirked. "Anyways, there can't be much meat on it."

Lard stood up so fast his chair slammed over backward. *"What'd you say?"*

Once Elsie and Mary-Jane stopped laughing and high-fiving each other, Elsie said, "You heard me."

Lard looked like he was about to release a cage of flying monkeys. "And you're nothing but a ruminant, polluting the atmosphere with your methane gas, who doesn't know that *anyways* isn't a real word!"

*Spoken like the son of a teacher*, Bones thought, scooting his cereal bowl slowly to the edge of his tray. His shoe waited in place. His socked foot tapped the floor while he waited to make his move. Then a cell phone went off in someone's pocket. All heads in the room swiveled as Elsie retrieved her phone, unsure if she should answer it or just hand it over.

Suddenly an orange peel flew past Bones's line of vision, then an empty milk carton. Elsie hollered, "Food fight!"

That gave Bones another idea. Maybe even better than the first one.

*No*, he told himself. *Stay focused.*

In the ensuing chaos, he dumped the soggy corn flakes into his shoe.

# 13

Bones had stopped breathing, afraid of getting busted or afraid of spilling his shoe, he wasn't sure which. He tried a neutral expression while lacing it back up. He felt Teresa watching him, as if adding up how many starving kids in China the contents of his shoe could feed.

She started to say something, then hesitated, and shook her head. Bones heard her mutter something after he'd gotten up to leave.

"I got T-A-L-L-C-H-I-E-F on a triple-word score," Alice said from the couch in the dayroom. The Scrabble board sat next to her on a cushion. Tiles were spread out in the empty box, all facing up. "You probably never heard of Maria Tallchief. She was the first Native American to be a prima ballerina."

"Cool." Bones shivered, mostly because his sock was wet. He limped over to check out the board. F-I-R-E-B-I-R-D. C-R-A-C-K-E-R. Alice chose three tiles from the box.

"Have you ever been to a ballet?" she asked, adding N-U-T to C-R-A-C-K-E-R.

"I'd like to someday."

"The classics are the best," she said. "I've been collecting old videos for years."

Then she smiled triumphantly. "Salt tablets."

At first he thought she was talking about her next play on the Scrabble board. "I quadrupled the dose to retain water," she explained.

Then Bones got it. "That'll give you five pounds of water weight."

"Just for weigh-in, then I'll pee it away," she said. "Chu Man may be smart, but I'm smarter. But don't try to hide soluble tablets in the tank behind the toilet. Even waterproof bags leak."

Bones nodded. There was so much she could teach him.

Alice twisted her hair into a Cinnabon on top of her head. "What is it about different body types shrinks don't understand? It's as if they want us all to look the same, like we should be pressed from the same mold. Seems a little Third Reich, if you ask me."

Bones knew what she meant. "Yeah."

"Have you ever seen a ballerina with an ounce of body fat?"

"You're the first real dancer I've met."

"A virgin." She smiled again, teasing him.

When she smiled at him like that it looked like a master had painted her. "The lighter we are—the higher we sail," she said. "How else can our partners lift us?"

She picked through the tiles and set G-I-S-E-L-L-E on the board. "This is the role that defines all classical ballerinas."

Nicole walked by sucking an orange wedge.

"Completely lacking self-control," Alice muttered.

"No willpower," Bones agreed.

"At least we have clear goals."

He nodded. "No one can call us quitters."

Nicole pretended like she hadn't heard them. "Bones," she said, ripping pulp with her teeth. "Your shoe is leaking."

Bones shrugged, trying to act nonchalant.

Nicole sauntered off.

"I was wondering," Alice said, "can you meet me in my room? Say in an hour?"

He was ready, willing, and able—for whatever she wanted.

· · · · · · · · · ·

Bones showered and changed into clean sweats. He sprayed Lard's aftershave on his shirt, then changed his mind. He was in the middle of swapping shirts when Lard came in.

"Thanks for sticking up for me," Bones said. "But Elsie isn't worth it."

"You can put up with some of the people some of the time"—Lard parked his lunchbox on his desk—"but not a domesticated ungulate."

Bones laughed. He'd called her a hoofed animal yet again. He went to the windowsill to check his shoe. Still wet.

Nancy appeared in the doorway, a bottle of Ensure in one hand, and a plastic cup in the other. Bones tried mild surprise. "What's up?"

She shook the bottle and her head in unison before unscrewing the cap. "This is to make up for the milk and cereal you dumped at breakfast."

*Busted!*

"How'd you know?"

Nancy poured, measuring carefully. "Do you mean besides the trail you left?"

Bones stepped backward, panic gnawing at him. "The milk I have for breakfast is nonfat," he said urgently. "And fifty calories from Ensure is from *fat*."

"Sorry, Bones. You made the kind of choice that didn't leave us with one." Nancy handed him the cup. "Dr. Chu ordered four ounces."

"BUT THE SCALES ARE SCREWED UP!"

. . . . . . . . . .

It was handy having Alice's room so close. Classical music filtered through the door, which was only open a few inches. Bones rapped softly, eased the door open, and knocked again.

"I've been waiting," Alice said.

Bones stepped inside.

Alice was sitting on the floor cutting strips of adhesive

tape off a roll. Her hair was still in a shiny bun but now ribbons were woven in. It was the first time he'd seen her in pink tights. They were as sexy as her ripped pair.

"This might seem like a crummy little hospital room," she said with a warm smile. "And, of course, it is. But it's also my studio while I'm stuck here, so I treat it like a temple. You know?"

"Sure."

"Lard told me about Elsie," she said. "I try to leave that kind of negative garbage outside."

He nodded again.

Bones didn't know why he was there or what to do with his hands. He shoved them in his pockets, playing with his gloves. Being alone with her like this was the closest he'd ever come to sex, even if they were both fully dressed.

Alice slipped a pad over her toes. "Gel pads," she explained. "I can't afford to lose any more toenails. After a while they don't grow back." She put on a pointe shoe, winding the ribbon around her ankle. Then she tied a knot and tucked in the loose ends. "At least I don't have bunions."

If she did, he'd kiss them away.

"With auditions coming up it's more important than ever that my technique is solid," she said, standing up. Her skirt moved restlessly around her thighs while she showed him how to use her video camera.

"Does Dr. Chu know you have this?"

"Yeah, a small concession." She shrugged. "Now try to keep it steady. Vertical, on my whole body."

"No problem," he said.

"You ready?" she asked.

"Yeah."

Bones hit record and watched through the viewfinder in wonderment and admiration as she defied the laws of physics. Her spine was straight as a shish kabob skewer, but when she bent her knees, she appeared to grow taller.

"*Pliés*," she explained the exercise. "Think of ballet as a play, but instead of learning lines, I memorize steps. I still have to act though, only as a dancer I use my whole body."

Bones thought about her actor parents. "Has your mom or dad been in any movies I'd know?" he asked, still filming.

"They're not famous, if that's what you mean. Except for being temperamental. Yelling and screaming to get their way or perfecting the cold shoulder. More of a cliché than a stereotype."

Alice balanced easily on one foot. "In ballet the audience sees one thing—the dancer. But they hear something else—the music." Her free foot made quick little flicks. "*Dégagés*," she said.

Bones squinted through the lens. "Sounds like a foreign language."

"It means to disengage. Like this, see? My foot releases from the floor. The terms are French, like the kiss."

Bones was grateful to be behind the camera. He wasn't used to this kind of attention. And it was definitely getting his attention below the waist.

"The audience brings its own energy, and that creates a whole new message," she said breathlessly, rising on her toes and turning gracefully. "I'm not just training to be a ballerina—I'm training my body to do whatever's asked of it."

Bones was lost in the sweat on her exquisitely sweating body. He was jealous of her sweat. He wanted to be her sweat. Even through the viewfinder he could see her ribcage pressing against her leotard like a musical instrument. He wanted to play her long into the night.

"What's going on in here?"

Bones nearly dropped the camera, turning to see Unibrow's massive head plugging the doorway.

Alice faced the brute, hands on defiant hips. "Did you even knock?"

"No exercising until—"

"I'm not exercising." She cut him off with a glare that could take down a gladiator. "I'm rehearsing."

"Not without permission from Dr. Chu." Unibrow glared right back. He was nothing but a no-neck jerk who thought he was better than them because he went home at night and slept on his own grimy sheets. "You know the rules better than anyone."

With that he left.

"I'd be so out of here if I had someplace to go." Alice worked pins from her bun, shaking out a tumble of strawberry blond. "The upcoming audition—that's my ticket." She poked his shoulder. "Come on, let's look at the video."

They sat side by side on the bed, her head tilted close to his. Escaped strands of hair brushed against him. It was *amazing*, more *amazing* than anything he'd ever felt. He watched her eighty-something pound presence on the screen. It was everywhere at once. "Amazing."

"Why didn't you tell me I was looking down?" She scolded him in such a way he had to sit on his hands to keep from shoving her backward on the bed and kissing her face. "That totally messes up my alignment. And look at that lousy extension."

Bones leaned in closer.

"I was lifting my hip during the *grand battements*. Even a three-year-old knows the hip is a ball and joint socket. It shouldn't move just because I raise my leg. All those days stuck in ICU and that stupid wheelchair." She sighed, pushing the envelope of impatience. "God, it's like I'm starting over."

He had to say it. "I think you look amazing."

And there was that smile again.

"Most people don't realize how strong ballerinas are because we look so fragile." She snapped the screen closed. "But we have to be strong, really strong, and I'm not just talking about physical strength. It takes a different kind of stamina to listen to someone scream at you hour after hour—"

"Your parents?"

"Well, yeah, like nonstop." She laughed. "But I meant the choreographer. Sometimes it's for the slightest thing, like a finger that isn't held just right. He's god—the creator and ruler and source of all power—the supreme being of the stage. Dancers? We're his puppets."

Bones was starting to realize that dancing wasn't just something she did; it was who she was.

Alice took his hand and pressed it on her chest just above her breast. "It comes from the core."

He tried to stay focused. "The heart?"

"Precisely."

Alice lifted one leg, untying her shoe.

"Need help taking the other one off?" he asked.

She leaned back on her pillow, holding her leg in the air.

Bones untied the satin knot carefully, until the ribbon fell, all crimped. He smoothed the wrinkles as best he could and set her shoes on the dresser.

It was time for Sexuality Group Therapy.

# 14

Alice had pulled a sweater over her damp leotard and was combing out her silky hair. Tape was still wrapped around her toes. Unfortunately, the arrangement of chairs didn't let them sit together. Lard was against the wall, rocking on the back legs of his chair. He sucked a toothpick, bored. Bones knew he'd rather be in the kitchen.

Bones avoided eye contact with Elsie, who looked like she'd spent the night under a train. She was talking to Sarah. "Once I was so sick I forgot to flush the toilet," she said. "Anyways, my mom saw the blood and figured out what I'd been doing."

That meant Elsie had ruptured something—probably her esophagus or stomach lining, Bones knew—because only a person sticking her finger down her throat several times a day threw up blood. He wondered if she had scars on her knuckles like the other VIs he'd met in groups like this.

"Our toilet kept overflowing," Sarah put in. "Pipes couldn't take whole chunks of food."

Lard's chair slammed the floor. "Can't you at least try to whisper?" he said, all edgy.

Elsie stood up ready for a fight and sat back down when Dr. Chu appeared. "Good afternoon, ladies and gentlemen. Thank you for being on time." Then he made a lame joke about the topic getting their attention.

"Anyways," Elsie said. "I've been on the pill since I was thirteen and my boyfriend uses condoms if that's what this is about."

Dr. Chu said something about responsibility being a sign of maturity and opened his briefcase. He passed out photographs of men and women of all ages. Some were in swimsuits, others in regular clothes. "Alice? How would you describe the women in these pictures?"

Except for a cute girl, Bones would have said fat, ugly, and lacking willpower. He wondered if Dr. Chu was going to hand out childproof scissors so they could cut out paper dolls to hang over their beds, a reminder of what normal should look like.

Alice was cool as a chilled cucumber. "Are you totally satisfied with your body, Dr. Chu? No, of course not. How do I know? Because no one is."

"That isn't the—" he started.

"Let's face it, you suffer from male pattern baldness, which explains the ponytail, and have an extraordinarily large nose." She stretched her amazing legs out in front of her. "Face it again, you'd like to lose those ten pounds you've put on since I saw you last summer."

"You're definitely a candidate for the lap band treatment," Mary-Jane told Dr. Chu.

Bones thought Dr. Chu may have seemed as calm as his Hallmark smile, but experience with shrinks told him the doctor was probably as uncomfortable as the rest of them.

Sure enough, Dr. Chu cleared his throat. "We all have target areas we'd like to change. But there comes a time when we have to look at ourselves in the mirror, smile, and say, 'Thank you for standing by me. For hanging in there after all the crap I've put you through.'"

"Explain this," Sarah said. "Anorexics think they're fat, right? Then why don't the rest of us think we're skinny?"

Lard snorted at that. "Cosmic injustice."

Alice looked up from braiding her hair. "Don't believe everything you think."

"I once had a shrink give me a piece of string and ask me to guess the size of my waist," Nicole said. "Then she measured me. I'd guessed my middle was fifteen inches smaller than it was. Talk about a wake-up call."

"Does anyone really have a healthy body image?" Mary-Jane asked.

"Our whole society is distorted," Nicole replied.

Elsie leaned forward with an expression that let them know they should pay attention. "Like this guy I know who dwells on his dangling participle, because he thinks it's larger than normal."

Mary-Jane and Nicole slapped high-fives.

"Anyways, take my boyfriend—" Elsie wouldn't give up.

Lard cut her off. "Sex addicts meet down the hall."

Dr. Chu let them talk, sort of like verbal free-writing. When things wound down, he gave them a bullshit assignment to sketch their bodies. "Just a simple outline," he said and dismissed the meeting. Then he asked to see Alice in his office. "Privately."

*Crap.* Unibrow must've ratted her out for rehearsing.

Bones watched everyone file out. Alice and Lard were the only people in the program with clearly defined goals. Alice would be a famous ballerina someday and Lard would have his own restaurant. Mary-Jane, Elsie, Nicole, Sarah, Teresa? They couldn't see past their next burger.

Bones admitted he hadn't had any aspirations about his future before checking into the hospital. Now he had one: Alice.

"I need your help in the kitchen," Lard told Bones in the hallway.

"Kitchens make me sick," Bones said.

"You're sick no matter where you are." Lard laughed and punched him in the arm.

Bones rubbed his wound. "Do I have to *eat* anything?"

"Nope."

"Touch anything?"

Lard shoved him toward the elevator. "Sure is tough being your friend."

The doors opened onto a world of aluminum appliances, all reflecting Bones's wavy image, a regular house of mirrors. The floor and counters looked like they'd gone through a carwash. You could eat off them if that was your thing.

Gumbo wore a bloody apron. He probably would have shaken Bones's hand, but he held a dead fish in one and a cleaver in the other. "The kitchen used to serve five floors," he said. "But now we only handle the EDU, obstetrics, and sometimes cater staff meetings."

Bones tried to look interested.

"I'm applying to this cooking school," Lard said, standing in front of the industrial size fridge. "My challenge is to get *fresh* back into school cafeterias without substituting watered-down ketchup for marinara sauce."

"It's an assignment?"

"Gorilla warfare." Lard nodded. "Here's the thing, man. I'm a compulsive overeater. I've always sneaked food, kept secret stashes, gorged when no one was around. Now I have a reason to be around food—a reason that makes me feel like I'm accomplishing something."

"Okay, I get it."

Lard took a cookie sheet from the fridge; it held two large pizzas. "This one's black bean nacho with roasted red peppers and jalapeños. And the other is your typical pineapple with smoked ham and glazed onions."

Bones stared at the mess, his stomach tying knots.

"Stop counting the goddamned calories," Lard said. "Just tell me which one looks the most appetizing."

"I hate beans."

Lard ignored him. "If you think about it, food is necessary for life. Ask anyone who's starved to death."

"Very funny," Bones said. Then he walked away, his stomach a tangled mess.

· · · · · · · · · ·

After a while Bones got used to Alice not being at every meal or every meeting. She kept getting called to different parts of the hospital for tests. She got mad if anyone asked about it because she hated being treated like she was sick.

"You think I like peeing in a bottle? Getting pricked with needles? Choking on potassium tablets?" she'd snap back. "I've given so much blood I'm anemic, so now they're giving me iron tablets, and if I ask for stool softeners, they accuse me of abnormal anxiety and unwarranted obsession over my bowels."

Nancy had appeared the last time to escort her downstairs. "Chest X-ray," she'd said. "Then an echocardiogram."

Bones knew that meant the doctors wanted to see how her heart was pumping.

With Alice downstairs and Lard in the kitchen, Bones asked Teresa if he could sit with her. "Sure," she said over a veggie burger fat enough to feed a family of four. "Did Lard show you his project?"

Bones nibbled his roll. "Yeah."

"I hope he gets into that school," she said, dipping a bite in barbecue sauce. "He's worked hard for it."

Bones chewed and chewed, churning his bite into dough. Then he faked a sneeze and spit into his napkin.

Teresa pretended she didn't see it.

"Do vegetarians eat animal crackers?" Elsie asked from across the room.

"Is Bud Wiser?" Mary-Jane retorted.

"Does his meat loaf?"

It went on like this for another five minutes.

After dinner Bones spent more time than usual breaking down tables and chairs. He kept hoping to see Alice. He finally gave up, went back to his room, and pulled out the letter he'd started writing to his sister. He'd added a couple of funny lines about Sex Therapy when Lard came in.

"That's the first and last time," Lard said, tossing a note to Bones. "I'm not a fucking carrier pigeon."

"Right. More like an aircraft carrier."

"Har. Har."

The note was from Alice. *Set your alarm clock for midnight and hide it under your pillow.*

Alice must have known the coast would be clear at that time, probably a change of shifts. Life was a lot easier when Unibrow wasn't on duty. His rubber soles were sometimes quiet as dust. He moved around the corridors, room to room, then materialized just when someone thought they might have a private moment.

As it turned out, Bones didn't need the alarm. Lard snored louder than usual. "Little Debbies," he kept saying in his sleep. Bones got up at 11:45, changed in the dark, and slipped inside Alice's room quiet as the laces in his Converse.

"Thanks for coming," she said softly.

Bones didn't see her at first. He turned toward her voice, letting his eyes adjust to the dull light. The moon broke through the curtains, shining yet full of shadows. She wore a dark leotard, tights, and leg-warmers. No skirt. She'd already put on her pointe shoes.

"I need help moving the bed," she whispered.

"Sure," he whispered back.

Bones scooted one side of the bed, then the other. Back and forth, it glided easily on wheels. Now she had room for her turns.

"*Fouettés*," she said. "It means to whip."

Bones stood there all nervous. He didn't know what to do—what she wanted him to do this time. "Anything else?"

"Just be my audience."

Bones stayed in the corner out of the way while she warmed up. She followed the same routine as before. After twenty minutes she started turning in place on one foot. Light and beautiful as an angel.

He counted silently. *One, two...nine, ten...* All on one amazing leg. He loved this, just being with her. Added bonus: staying up burned more calories than sleeping.

Without taking a breath, Alice repeated the same

number of turns on her other leg. Then she asked him if he'd partner her, unsure of what that meant.

"Stand behind me," she said. "Put your hands here, on the sides of my waist."

Bones touched the thin layer of spandex. "Here?"

"Yes, like that. Lightly," she said, "You don't have to hold me up—just use your hands like a guide. It helps me stay centered."

Touching her like this felt like a gift. It was so real. He had to force himself to ignore everything that was going on inside and concentrate on the task. Alice began to turn with even more confidence than she'd had on her own. *Twelve... thirteen, fourteen...* He knew this was the strength she'd been talking about. *Sixteen, seventeen...* She could dance all night if she wanted to. *Eighteen, nineteen, twenty...* If Dr. Chu could see her like this he'd stop ordering all those tests.

Alice landed silently as a feather. She stretched out on the floor, then slid into the splits, grabbed her ankle, and pulled herself down even farther. "Press against my lower back."

Bones knelt down, pressing his palms into the hollow above her butt.

She sighed and bent forward even more. "Yeah, that's the spot."

He felt dampness through her leotard as she relaxed into the stretch. Alice smelled so good. So fresh, so real, so alive. He didn't know how else to think about her.

*Alive.*

"Push a little harder," she said. "Don't worry, you can't hurt me."

They were quiet for a while and then she asked Bones to get the Preparation H from the bathroom.

He didn't turn on the light until he was inside in case someone was outside in the hall. He looked around quickly; ribbons and scarves hung over her towel rack. The tube Lard had given her lay on the sink beside a bottle of baby oil.

Bones turned off the light and went back to his love. He sat beside her on the floor and rubbed Prep H into her feet, happier than ever at being able to help her.

At 2 a.m. they lingered awhile for a last good-night.

· · · · · · · · · ·

Moonlight muted his room.

Bones lay in bed with his eyes closed, visualizing the sheen of Alice's smooth skin. Her long legs. The nape of her neck. Eyes opened, staring at the ceiling, or eyes closed. It didn't matter. Not even Lard's snoring could block the image or feel of her tiny waist in his hands.

And there she was, a vision of sexiness floating through his window, asking if she could spend the night with him. He drifted off thinking about all the things she'd do to him under the sheets. Love. Pure love. Bones awoke, wet and sticky. "Are you kidding me?"

Lard stirred in his bed. "What now?"

"Someone squirted Elmer's glue on my..." he said,

joking to keep from being embarrassed. "Either that or I'm dying and my brains are leaking out."

"You got it wrong, man," Lard chuckled. "Beating off causes blindness."

"Is that why you wear glasses?" Bones shot right back. He got to his feet, stripping to his skivvies.

Lard swung his legs over the side of his bed and sat up. "Better add more protein to your diet."

Bones hit the shower still in his skivvies. He soaped them up and stripped all the way. He hung his skivvies to dry, toweled off, and got dressed.

"Nancy stopped by," Lard said when Bones came out. "Thought we might want to straighten up our room in case our parents want a tour."

Bones had nearly forgotten: Family Therapy Night.

# 15

Bones hadn't really lied to his parents about important things, though he'd kept a million little secrets about what he thought about himself on a good day (crap) or on a bad day (shit)—and the myriad of disgusting things he'd done to lose weight. If the omission of truth equaled lies, then he was a fabricator extraordinaire.

An hour before moms and dads, sisters and brothers, and various other relatives were expected to be *fully present and in the here and now*, Bones was in his room watching Lard stalk a daddy longlegs with a piece of toilet paper.

Lard dropped on it. "Bull's-eye!"

"You can't be that hungry," Bones said.

"I'm telling you, man, these family meetings can be a real clusterfuck." Lard tossed the wad out the open window.

Bones pulled on his gloves. He'd been in endless meetings with his parents and sister and dubious therapists but never with other kids and their families and therapists.

Who knew what to expect? Guess he'd play along like always, which seemed the least he could do considering the program was ridiculously expensive—forty-five hundred dollars a week. The twenty-seven thousand dollars paid by his dad's health insurance could have covered a year's tuition, room, and board at a state university.

..........

Dr. Chu was rushing around like an energetic host. "There's nothing to worry about," he kept saying.

Bones didn't know who he was talking to, but it was nerve-wracking when an obnoxiously imperious adult felt the need to reassure him about something. Bones figured the question marks on Dr. Chu's tie were significant in some Freudian way.

The room looked like someone's idea of a party. Raw vegetables marched around a bowl of yogurt dip. A pitcher of lemonade stood by a platter of lemon-iced cookies. Coffee. Nondairy creamer. Sugar cubes. A little universe of sugar and fat. Something for people to do with their hands.

Lard parked himself by the couch, rolling a toothpick between his fingers, as if trying to decide who to stab first. Teresa had removed the safety pin from her face. She looked better without it, almost pretty.

Bones turned when Alice walked in. She took his breath away, literally, in a sundress with skinny shoulder straps. She wore flat sandals and a delicate gold anklet. Flowers were woven into her hair, which fell softly around her shoulders.

Almond eyes and strawberries. Add whipped cream and a cherry. Bones wanted to cover her like chocolate sauce, a forbidden sundae.

And in they came.

All looking as anxious as mice in a trap. Hugs first. Polite introductions next. Bones knew some of them had traveled a long way to be here. More than one of the girls warned her family in whispers about Dr. Chu's propensity to lecture.

Teresa's mom was plump with the same cocoa complexion and nervous hands. She filled a paper plate with cookies. Her dad stood back, looking uncertain. Elsie's mom was too gaudy in DayGlo for the dreary room. Elsie didn't have a dad; at least, he wasn't here. Her brother seemed normal enough in cargo pants and an AzHiAzlaM T-shirt. Sarah and Nicole seemed genuinely excited to see their families. Mary-Jane welcomed her grandparents.

Lard's mom came by herself. She was short and squat, wearing wide horizontal stripes, like she wanted to show off her size. She kissed Lard on the cheek and gave him a plastic sack. "A new apron."

"Thanks, Mom." Lard kissed her, taking the bag. Then he introduced her to Bones.

Bones could tell she was nice.

She smiled. "Bones?"

He shrugged. "Yeah."

Lard said the cookies were sugar and fat-free. "So you can eat as many as you want."

Lard's mom smiled again, and Lard smiled back, and Bones realized how much Lard liked her. Dr. Chu kept adjusting his smile, shaking hand after hand like an overzealous politician.

Alice moved across the room toward a couple that had to be her parents. They wore expensive-looking suits. Hers, beige silk. High heels. His, white linen. Tom's slip-ons, no socks. Both had practiced smiles and spray-on tans. They converged on Alice with air kisses.

Alice was right. It was like they were actors playing the part of caring parents.

Bones was beginning to worry that his parents were stuck in traffic when they finally walked in, looking as uncertain as everyone else.

"Jack!" His parents rushed past the others.

Bones nearly lost it and trembled when they pulled him into a hug, letting his arms drape over their shoulders. They felt like home and all the things he missed, even his dad's stubbly cheek. He knew his mom would cry but didn't expect his dad's wet eyes. "We know it isn't easy being in here," his dad whispered. "We want you to know how proud we are."

When they pulled apart, his sister said, "The house is a big empty planet without you, weirdo." Her smile could polish the room. She had on Bones's North Face beanie, the one with the moth hole.

Bones was about to ask his mom about the brown bag she was holding when Dr. Chu told everyone to find a seat.

Elsie looked like she couldn't wait to get this party started. Teresa looked like she couldn't wait for it to end.

"I'll begin with a general explanation of eating disorders," Dr. Chu said. "Then we'll open it up to questions. Tonight's gathering is as much for the families as for the patients."

Everyone waited for him to go on.

"These disorders often begin with a typical preadolescent fixation on appearance," Dr. Chu said, showing off a few thousand dollars of knowledge. He glanced around the room, staring into people's eyes until they had to look away or die. "That soon turns into habits, patterns, and finally becomes an obsession."

They'd heard it all before. Their families had heard it. But the good doctor seemed compelled to repeat it for those who may have suffered from chronic memory loss.

He stood center stage in a theater in the round, never missing an opportunity to give an audience something to digest.

"Food or the control of food makes up for feelings that may otherwise seem overwhelming…food becomes a means of communication or solace or stillness."

Elsie's mom got up for more cookies.

Alice's mom opened her purse and absently checked her cell phone. No messages apparently. She made a face and her lips pooched out, like she was channeling Donald or Daffy.

Lard cleared something gross from his throat. "Maybe someone else would like to talk."

Dr. Chu raised an accusing eyebrow at Lard. This wasn't part of his script. "Yes, of course, Mr. Kowlesky. Does anyone have something to share?"

The room grew so quiet you could have heard a tissue drop. Lard's mom reached for one. Even the board games on the shelf were paying attention. It was like the moment after a pop quiz is announced when no one knows the answers. The room was a heart that had misplaced its beat.

Then someone coughed.

"Teresa?" Dr. Chu said. "Would you like to talk about your recent breakthrough?"

Teresa played with the eyebrow that used to have a safety pin. She glanced around, obviously uneasy about talking in front of a room of strangers. "I've been losing weight in a healthy way," she said quietly.

"Anything else?" Dr. Chu asked.

She looked down, knowing what he was asking. "I was molested," she muttered into her chest.

Her mom grabbed her sleeve. "Shhh. *Siéntate. Cállate.*"

Lard looked about to lose it. "Let her talk."

Tick-tock.

Fun and games were over.

Teresa pulled away from her mom. She began telling her story, talking really fast. "After school by our neighbor…"

As Teresa continued, every so often she would shiver then sob. Tissues were passed. When she finished, her dad said, "I told you not to speak about that. *Nunca, niña.*"

His words were a karate chop.

Teresa collapsed farther into her chair

The room stared at Dr. Chu, waiting for him to say something. Do something. For Teresa. But it was Nancy who sprang into action. In an instant she was by Teresa's side, talking to her softly, soothing her, without actually touching her.

Then Mary-Jane's grandmother spoke up. "You act like your daughter did something wrong, as if being molested was her fault. You're the one who should be standing beside her, supporting her."

"Believing in her," Lard's mom added.

Teresa wiped her eyes.

Lard snapped his toothpick. "The worst thing a parent can do is try to quiet her kid when she's ready to talk about something like this."

Teresa sniffed, sucking it up.

Elsie pushed herself out of her chair. "The second worst thing she can do is put her down in a room full of goddamned people!"

"You can't make something like that disappear," Nicole threw in. "Just because you don't talk about it doesn't mean it never happened."

Bones knew it often occurred like this. He'd seen lots of families who smiled too hard under the strain of trying to act normal in group meetings. Then a hurtful word or glance and someone cracked and spoke out of turn. Pretty soon even adults were acting inappropriately.

Jill leaned into his shoulder. Bones took off his gloves and held his sister's hand.

Then Alice's dad stood up. He walked purposefully toward the cart and poured himself a cup of coffee, stirring in sugar without letting the spoon touch the side of the cup. His tanned brow glistened. A dot of sweat darkened his lapel.

He blew on his coffee and turned to address Dr. Chu. "Do you really know any more about this disease than the rest of us?"

Alice's mom cringed as if her husband had just thrown up and she didn't want to get splattered. The rest of the room swiveled, like it was seeing the aftermath of a terrible accident and couldn't look away.

Bones expected Dr. Chu to rise to the argument. Instead he kept his gaze even, as if trying to prove this was a democratic forum where all voices would be heard.

Alice's dad continued. "You don't know what it's like having hopes and dreams for your only child," he said with a theatrical intake of air. "And realizing they'll never materialize because she's sick and not getting better."

Whatever Dr. Chu was planning to say next seemed to be causing him great pain.

Alice's dad stirred the life out of his coffee while boxes of tissues were passed. "You don't have any idea how many times she's been in and out of hospitals like this." His voice boomed, trained to reach the balcony. "Programs like this, even the unconventional, alternative ones."

"Please, Mr. Graham, let's not talk about this here," Dr. Chu said evenly. "We can discuss it later, in private."

Alice shrank into herself, slid like a shadow from her chair, and floated down the hall toward her room. Bones watched her go, dying bit by bit. He wanted to kidnap Alice. Take her away from here. Hold her. Be there for her. But he just sat there paralyzed like everyone else.

Lard glared at Dr. Chu. "I thought the reason families are here tonight is so we can talk about all kinds of stuff—"

Nicole picked it up. "Instead of using food like we have in the past to stuff our feelings so we're more dependent on food than ever to make us feel better."

"Like right now I'd sell my soul for a bucket of tater tots and a keg of beer." Elsie scanned the room, daring anyone to make her shut up. "How does that make you feel anyways?"

Bones liked that everyone in the ward was sticking up for everyone else. And they seemed genuinely concerned for Alice's fragile condition. Her dad was still standing, his posture a challenge. "Can anyone tell me if there's a cure for this damn disease?"

*Eating disorder,* Bones wanted to shout at him. *Not disease.* Cancer is a disease. Tuberculosis is a disease. Chicken pox is a disease. It even sounded like something with a scab that can scar you for life. Food is a...*what*? A nutritional substance needed to maintain life. *Whoa!* Did that really come from him?

Dr. Chu raised his hand as though to forestall a riot.

Then he took a step backward, as if expecting overturned chairs, flailing fists, flying coffee cups. He started to say something then changed his mind and finally took over, trying to calm people down, talking to parents and other family members individually.

*Difficult time.*

*Understandably upset.*

*Recovery can be painful.*

*Conquer your fears.*

Everyone seemed unaware of the others.

As soon as it was obvious that the meeting had ended, people began standing up, glancing nervously from Dr. Chu to the boxes of tissues on the floor to the platter of sugarless cookies. Bones ushered his parents and sister down the hall to his room. Lard had at least attempted to make his bed.

Jill studied the bulletin boards. "Cozy little warzone in there," she said, referring to the meeting. "Not what I expected."

His mom looked equally disturbed. "Why do people have to argue like that?" She shrugged, kneading the brown bag. "And those two girls. What was the tiny one's name?"

Knives diced his heart. "Alice."

"All you have to do is look at her," his dad said, "to know it wouldn't take much to push her over the edge."

"How could her dad talk about her like she wasn't even there?" Jill put in. "What's the point of bringing up past failures?"

Bones thought about Alice slinking down the hall to escape her dad's outburst. How no one had tried to stop her. Not her parents, Dr. Chu, or Nancy. Bones felt horrible, imagining Alice alone in her room, lost in ballet exercises, tuning out the world and everyone in it.

He couldn't imagine having insensitive parents like hers. His mom and dad loved each other as much as they loved him and his sister, even if they could be OCD when it came to work. At least they weren't hooked on prescription meds or irresponsible with credit cards, like some of his friends' parents. No sadistic sexual rituals with dead chickens.

He felt guilty all over again, because as much as he told his family everything was okay, he'd noticed the dark circles under his mom's eyes and his dad's distressed glances during the meeting when he didn't know Bones was watching.

Bones half-expected his family to say something about Rachael Ray's poster over Lard's bed—or to ask how he liked his roommate or if he'd put on weight or how he liked the food. But they didn't say any of those things.

His mom only wanted to know if he needed anything from home. She set the bag on his bed and pulled out toothpaste, socks, and plastic hangers. "What do you think, honey?" she asked, shaking out a pair of jeans.

Bones hadn't worn jeans since the sixth grade. They were too tight out of the clothes dryer, pliers pinching his waist. He hated their sandpaper stiffness. "Thanks, Mom," he said.

His dad wanted to know if he'd been following baseball on TV. "Looks like the Dodgers have a shot at the pennant." Then he gave him a couple of twenties for incidentals.

Jill was flipping through Lard's cookbooks. "Are these your roommate's?"

"Yeah," Bones said. "He wants to have his own restaurant."

The irony was not lost on her. "Slick."

"He's a great guy."

That was enough for them; it was time to say good-bye.

Bones watched his family go, more worried than ever about Alice.

# 16

Bones glanced at the clock. Eight minutes past ten. Lights out. Where was Lard? He put on his wool beanie and checked the hall for squeaky soles. The ward was shadows and suspiciously quiet. How could anyone sleep after what happened earlier?

He slipped unseen through the dayroom and headed to the stairs.

· · · · · · · · · ·

There was enough light from the moon shining on the roof to see Alice, Lard, and Teresa huddled together on chairs under the same blanket. It smelled like a pot-smoker's convention. Bones heard Alice sigh and saw the red tip of a cigarette waving back and forth like a gold sparkler.

Lard's flashlight blinked an SOS. "What took you so long, man?"

Bones wondered how many rules they were breaking by being up here so late. Lard and Teresa getting high. Alice smoking like a chimney. He must've said it aloud because Teresa just about snapped his head off.

"I don't give a crap about rules anymore," she said and fanned smoke before passing the joint back to Lard.

Bones dragged a chair over. "No problem, Teresa. I totally get it."

"It's always anorexia and bulimia around here, like A, B," Lard said, exhaling loudly. "Seems like a little S and M might be a nice change."

Teresa thumped him.

Alice offered Bones a corner of the blanket, and he burrowed in under the watchful eyes of tomatoes, beans, and squash. She clutched a slow-burning Marlboro; the cigarette trembled in her fingers.

"You okay?" he asked her.

"Same controlling bullshit," she said softly. "Different day."

Alice took a deep drag and filled her lungs. Her body loved it. Bones loved it too. Suddenly he was jealous of the smoke.

"It's your turn, Lard," Alice said.

Lard giggled like a little kid. "Uh, what was the question?"

"You're already stoned," she said.

He held his hands up in mock peace. "Oh, yeah, I remember. *Truth*."

"What's your favorite animal?" she asked.

Lard paused. "Spareribs."

"I like it." Alice's voice smiled. "And what's the most embarrassing thing you've ever done?"

"Got caught pissing in a bathroom sink," he said, staring into nothingness. "But I was drunk."

That got a laugh.

Alice's breath was visible in the night air. She lit another cigarette with the one she was smoking. "Teresa?"

"Truth, I, uh, think. Uh, yeah, I'm totally good with reality." She sounded as stoned as Lard, until she said, "Unlike every other person in my family."

They were quiet for a while, then Alice said, "Tell us one thing you don't like about each of us."

Teresa burrowed in closer to Lard. "Okay, this is for Bones. Promise you won't get mad."

"Lay it on me," Bones said.

"I don't like the way you watch me eat—like I'm some kind of freak for trying to be healthy."

Lard nodded. "Sometimes you come off as a contemptuous asshole," he said. "But I mean that kindly."

They laughed again.

Then they were quiet again. So peaceful. No one bugging them. Just them, being. Bones was thinking their little game had more truth in it than what had gone on downstairs. "Alice." Teresa paused, unsure if she should go on. "I don't like the way you use people to get what you want—"

"Now who's being patronizing," Alice said.

"Hey," Lard said. "Not nice."

Teresa didn't back down. "We just want you to get well."

"I got enough of that earlier," Alice said. She stubbed out her cigarette and lit another one with little thought to the combustible material of the blanket. Even in the fuzzy light Bones could see her face was flushed.

Teresa was back in the game. "There's only one thing I don't like about Lard. I'm afraid he doesn't like me as much as I like him." She relaxed into his shoulder, and grinned, big and goofy, like she couldn't believe what she'd just said.

Lard sat there, stoned and stunned. His joint burned on its own. Then he took Teresa's hand and they slid from underneath the blanket and disappeared into the darkness. A light wind ruffled across the roof. Alice snuggled closer to Bones, barely smoking her cigarette. Bones watched it smolder. "What's your wildest fantasy?" she asked, suddenly looking at him.

Alone in the dark, hunched in conspiracy, this was his chance to admit how he saw their future together. But here was the thing: Bones was half afraid he was too inexperienced for her, even though the other half of him was on fire by what he was feeling.

So he lied.

He talked into the blanket so he wouldn't have to see her eyes when he told her his second wildest fantasy. "I'm sick of being sick," he said.

Alice acted like that's what she suspected all along. "God, Bones, don't let them suck you in."

"It isn't like that," he said. "Lately I've been wondering what it would be like if I wasn't so freaked out by food."

She looked at him, clearly disappointed. "You'd be like everyone else."

Bones nearly backed down. But if he didn't get it out now, he never would. "There'd be all this room in my head for other things to obsess about," he said. "It might be fun to find out what they'd be."

They got up and walked to the edge of the roof, peering through the chain-link fence. Bones shivered inside his sweats and wool beanie. His eyes watered. His nose ran. He sniffled while connecting stars into mythical monsters. It would've been scary if the sky wasn't so beautiful. Bones couldn't believe no one else was with them to see it. Alice seemed just as mesmerized.

Even though they stood close to each other, he felt like he was on the outside of a snow globe, admiring her perfection inside. Alice must've sensed him staring at her because she started telling him stuff, and it was like they were stepping into the most magical part of their relationship, and in the sharing, the magic was bringing him slowly inside the globe with her.

"My mom was pissed when she got pregnant and not just because she gained sixty pounds. Stretch marks and sagging boobs were a serious setback in her career," she said. "My parents never forgave me for choosing ballet over acting. It's hard to explain to someone who doesn't dance, but it's like being in another world. Just me and the music."

She stood still and played with the fringe on her scarf. "Nothing else matters, Bones. *Nothing.* Not eating or sleeping or parents with screwed-up priorities or grades and all that school bullshit."

He used to feel that way about lifting weights. Just him alone in his bedroom, head to toe in heavy fleece, space heaters cranked on high. Now that's how he felt about Alice. She mattered more than anything.

Her biggest secret, she said, was that she'd pretended to be the perfect daughter while really hating her mom and dad, and they pretended to be perfect parents while being unforgiving of her failures, and her biggest fear of all was that she'd end up being just as phony as they were.

"You could never be—"

She stopped him. "It's okay, Bones, I know who I am."

They stood there for a while in the crisp night without talking. Below, streetlamps glowed amber. Brake lights flashed. An ambulance screamed by. Just being with her like this made him happy. He didn't know what to say anyway.

"There's a bus stop in front of the hospital," Alice said, pressing into him. "You can go just about anywhere from here."

Bones pressed back. Being aroused could be so awkward.

"Wouldn't it be fun to get on a bus and not know where you'd end up?" she asked.

Bones didn't answer because he wasn't sure if she was inviting him. He willed his arm upward, letting it hover over her shoulder, wanting to touch her, but not sure he should. He hoped she wouldn't turn abruptly, and lose an eye to his elbow.

She turned to him abruptly. Even in the dark her gaze was intense. "I'm either in class or rehearsing for a studio performance or exhausted from class and rehearsing and sleeping. It's like that twenty-four-seven. I don't have time for anything else. But if I ever thought it was possible to have—you know, a boyfriend..."

Bones tried to appear nonchalant, but the word *boyfriend* had so much power he knew he was in danger of tripping, falling through the fence, dropping headfirst ten stories to the sidewalk. Another Romeo bites the dust.

"And not just because I think skinny is sexy." She shivered against the cold. "But because you're skinny *and* cute."

They strolled back to the chairs and snuggled under the same blanket and the astonishingly romantic sky—her smoking and him not doing anything but thinking how much he loved her—and on fire because she'd just called him sexy.

"I had your room last summer," she said quietly.

That set off a whole new set of fantasies in his head.

"I hid something in there. Could you look for me?"

"Sure, what is it?"

"Blank hospital menus," she said.

Bones knew the significance of having something like that. "Where did you get them?"

"Someone I hung out with."

Bones felt a twinge of jealousy wondering who'd take such a risk for her.

"I wrapped them in plastic," she said.

Lard and Teresa ambled back to the chairs holding hands. Lard's glasses had fogged up. He wiped them repeatedly. His hulk of a body was overheated and making endless steam.

No one asked what time it was, but they knew they had to go back. Bones wanted to walk Alice to her room, sit with her in the dark, stroke her hair until she fell asleep. But he knew it was safer if they split up. Alice and Teresa took the elevator. Bones and Lard headed for the stairs.

The EDU was a tomb. Their room dark. Lard hit the bed hard, kicking off his boots and stripping to his shorts. "Teresa and I might be a couple. I like to cook and she likes to eat. It doesn't get any better than that."

With that he was asleep, a buzz saw in need of WD-40.

. . . . . . . . . .

The depressing part of waking up to the sun blasting through a summer window was knowing you couldn't hit the beach. Lard woke up slowly and growled, a bear coming out of hibernation. "My mouth tastes like the inside of an old shoe." He muttered his way to the bathroom.

Bones had already been up for an hour searching for

the blank menus Alice had mentioned. He'd checked the underside of both beds, thinking she might have wedged them between the mattress and box springs. He'd shined a light on the inside of the closet door and checked behind Lard's bulletin board, where he found another piece of CRAP.

Near the opening above his family's unit, Calvin heard the unmistakable melody of a human voice. Who else would defy the curfew ordinance? He dared to ask, "Who's there?"

No answer.

Calvin swung off his bike, worked the front wheel into the rubble. "It's okay," he said. "I'm CRAP. Like certifiably."

Then he saw her. A girl about his age, lying on her back with arms crossed over her chest. What shocked him most was the neglect of her uniform, which appeared to be sending a message to His Excellence—UP YOURS—a phrase a kid in his History Is Dead class used.

Calvin smiled at the girl. "Are you okay?"

She moaned.

"What's your name?"

Finely spun hair framed the most exquisite face he'd ever seen. But her eyes were grave, staring. He'd seen that expression but had never figured out if it was hope, longing, or fear. Her unruly presence gave him courage to talk to her.

"Are you CRAP?"

She moaned louder and sank into herself.

"Lard!" Bones called.

Lard stuck his head out of the bathroom, holding the side of his neck. "You better not be messing with Woody!"

"Nah, Buzz is my man. So listen to this." He read him the first few paragraphs. "I've been finding pages like this all over the ward. Who do you think wrote it?"

"George was working on a novel," Lard said. "Is it science fiction?"

"Yeah. Why would he hide it?"

"Maybe so Dr. Chu wouldn't find it?" Lard said, still clutching his neck. "Do you have any self-tanner?"

"Nah, it turns my skin orange."

Lard dropped his hand, revealing a hickey.

Bones laughed. "How about a Band-Aid?"

"Okay."

Dr. Chu had called a special meeting so they could process what had happened during the snafu of Family Night. Predictably, he wanted them to express their feelings. But everyone was too emotionally rung out. As a consolation he asked if they had any grievances.

Elsie was quick to point out how ridiculous it was to go to bed at ten o'clock on weekends. Dr. Chu very generously agreed to extend lights out to eleven on Saturday nights. But when asked if they could sleep in Sunday mornings, he said, "We'll see," which always meant no.

# 17

Three days had passed since Bones and Alice, Lard and Teresa had hung out on the roof. If Dr. Chu knew they had sneaked out after curfew, he didn't call them on it. Maybe he thought they needed to decompress after such a FUBAR of a family session and trusted them enough to know they hadn't left hospital grounds. Or maybe he needed to decompress himself.

Bones's sister sent him one of those antiquated communications systems known as a postcard. It pictured a sprawling orange grove. *When life sucks like lemons, hold out for Florida oranges. He found a funny one in the gift shop. I don't suffer from insanity, I enjoy it.*

Other than therapy sessions and endless writing exercises that began *Dear Fear, Dear Fat*, or *Dear Comfort Food* and great mental anguish during meals, Bones spent most of his free time helping Alice prepare for her audition. He could tell she was growing stronger every day.

"I won't be a principal dancer at first," she'd explained one afternoon in her room. "But that's okay, as long as I'm dancing."

Bones filmed.

Alice critiqued.

She explained the French names of movements with a pure and radiant smile that glistened with sweat. *Battement* meant to beat. *Piqué* to prick. *Port de bras* wasn't what Bones had hoped—as in, does it hook in font or in back? It meant how the arms moved.

After lights out, sometimes at two in the morning, sometimes three or four depending on the night staff and whether or not it was Unibrow, Bones moved Alice's bed so she had room to turn.

One night she showed up in his room in the dark. "Wake up, Bones," she said, shaking him gently. "Follow me—I need a back rub."

Another night he and Alice sneaked out of the ward and down the back stairs. They were nearly spotted in the lobby by a security guard but Alice saw him first. "Quick!" she whispered, dragging Bones into a storage room. They huddled in the dark listening to the sound of fading footsteps. Then Bones filmed her in front of the gift shop while she did amazing leap things. Mannequins smiled through tempered glass.

Before saying good night, he'd hold her hummingbird feet while she did crunches. Afterward she'd ride his back while he sweated out push-ups. Each *tête–à–tête* filled him with longing. He knew Alice was part of him and always would be. He'd been put on this planet to be with her.

"Was it good for you?" she asked, collapsing from exhaustion.

His cup runneth over.

. . . . . . . . . .

The next weigh-in was worse than the first.

The room was a walk-in freezer.

Bones was a block of ice.

This time he was commando under his gown. Utterly defenseless. No weight belt, stainless steel cutlery, or lead pellets lurking in his seams. He pinched the back of his gown further embarrassed because Nancy was in charge of his exam.

"Take a deep breath and let it out slowly," she said, stethoscope pressed against his chest. "You okay?"

He couldn't stop shaking. "Sure."

She slapped a blood pressure cuff on his arm, took his temperature, made a note, and told him to step on the scales. Fear tangled his legs, trying to crush his bones. What if he'd gained weight? Worse still, what if he'd lost weight? Then Dr. Chu would raise his calories even more. A lose-lose situation.

Nancy touched his arm gingerly. "One small step..."

Bones closed his eyes against bold numbers. He stepped up, froze. Metal burned the soles of his feet. The sound of clicking rattled in his ears. Little bullets aimed at his brain. What kind of lies would the scales tell this time?

"Dr. Chu will be pleased," she said.

Bones stepped down, shivering. Nancy had returned the sliding weight to zero. "How much?" he asked.

"Dr. Chu will go over the results with you."

"Can't you tell me?"

"Sorry, Bones."

"But it's my body," he said.

"You'll have to talk to the doctor."

What did that mean?

..........

Bones didn't want to think about his body fat or fat body and he sure as shit didn't want to talk about it. He was more than willing to join a particularly vicious game of Scrabble in the dayroom.

Lard and Teresa were nestled on the couch intense over their tiles. Alice sat cross-legged in the easy chair; her ballet skirt hiked over her knees. She frowned, thumbing through the Scrabble dictionary. "I know *derriere* is a word."

Lard looked up. "What's that, Spanish?"

"French," she said. "As in, I tripped over one of your bad jokes and fell on my *derriere*."

Teresa added an *R, E,* and *Y* to Lard's C-O-V-E-R making it R-E-C-O-V-E-R-Y. "Twenty-three points," she said. "Your turn, Bones. And Alice? Foreign words don't count."

Alice shrugged, deep in the dictionary.

"I don't know why you cheat," Lard said. "You'd beat us anyway."

"*Battement*," Bones said the French word meaning beating.

Alice grinned at him. "Impressive."

"Cheating," Lard repeated.

"It's not cheating." Her smoked almond eyes scanned the board. "Just implementing creative strategy."

Bones focused on his *X*. O-X, A-X-E, or C-O-X. He needed an *N* for A-N-O-R-E-X-I-C, which would move his score closer to Alice's, and more importantly, thoroughly impress her with his skill and intelligence.

Bones counted the *N*s on the board. "Pass," he said, turning in three tiles. He drew a *T, S,* and a blank. T-O-X-I-C S-E-X.

"Guess what?" Alice told Bones. "I found those blank menus I told you about. Apparently furniture was moved around a couple of months ago during an E. coli outbreak."

"Most strains are harmless," Lard said.

"So hey," she said, leaning into Lard. "I need a favor."

He took off his glasses and worked at a particularly stubborn smudge. A high-calorie-food byproduct, no doubt. "Forget it."

Alice pulled a menu from her journal and laid it on the board. It was obvious she'd filled it out herself: vegetable broth, 15 calories; strawberry Jell-O, 14 calories; 1 saltine cracker, 13 calories. "Just substitute it for tomorrow's dinner."

"That's a starvation diet, Alice," Lard said, reading from the sheet. "As in *suicide*."

"It's my body," she said. "Besides, do you think I'd hurt myself? With auditions coming up?"

He shook his head. "You can't live on this."

"Just another five pounds," she said in a voice that was both entreating and vulnerable.

"Right. Then another five. Same old story and you're back in ICU. Sorry, Alice, I'm not Dr. Kevorkian."

"What do you know about it? You think it's easy to train without a studio? That'd be like you trying to cook without a stove. Shit, I don't even have a decent mirror, and I have to use the bed for a barre."

"Fame..." he muttered.

"Now who's being a pompous ass?" Alice dumped her tiles on the board before knocking the whole thing on the floor. "Sometimes I just hate you!"

"Yeah, well." Lard stood up quietly. "Teresa, wanna help prep dinner?"

Teresa studied the scattered alphabet, evidence of how quickly life on the ward could turn sour. "Okay."

"God, I need a cigarette," Alice said after they left. She leaned forward and her leotard stretched even tighter over her chest. "I bet you wouldn't have said no if you worked in the kitchen."

"Uh, well, no."

"You mean you'll do it?" She appeared to be deciding

exactly what to say before saying it. "If you get caught, you're toast."

"I won't get caught."

Her dark eyes danced. "Really?"

"Clandestine is my middle name."

"An extremely attractive trait." Alice smiled, fresh and radiant. "Gumbo keeps this box on the kitchen counter. Inside is a file with all of our menus. Signed, sealed, and delivered by Chu Man himself. It shouldn't be that hard to swap them."

And Bones knew just how he'd do it.

. . . . . . . . . .

An hour before lunch the next day Bones stepped into the noisy, stinky steam of the kitchen with its violently hissing pots. It smelled like something that had been dead too long. Cattle, pigs, chicken, fish, all of the above.

"If you're here to complain that the food is overpriced or the service is too slow or…" Lard shot over his shoulder.

"The portions are too big," Bones said, scanning the cluttered counter. His eyes stopped on the file box of menus sitting by the cookbooks. Not exactly in plain sight, but not hidden either. He'd have to be careful. If Lard caught him he'd be cooked alive.

Gumbo shouted at Lard from a chopping block. "Rinse the pasta!"

Bones got out of the way while Lard tugged on oven mitts and grabbed an enormous pot. In one slick move he dumped the pot into a strainer and cranked the cold water handle. "What's up?" he asked.

Bones shifted his weight hoping to seem his usual obsessive self. "Something's assaulting the green beans in the garden. Like, seriously."

Lard turned, his face red and sweaty. "What can I do about it?"

"Looks like a scourge, maybe red-bellied beetles," Bones said, feigning concern. "Once the beans are wiped out the little bastards will move on to the tomatoes."

Bones registered a flash of panic in Lard's eyes. "I could make a spray," he said quickly. "Black pepper with dish soap should do it."

"Spray bottles are on a shelf by the freezer," Gumbo hollered out.

While Lard and Gumbo sliced and diced in a frightening frenzy, Bones filled a spray bottle with water and poured in soap. When the other two were at the stove tossing veggies in frying pans, he did what Alice had asked, swapping the menus she'd filled out with the official ones.

Which as it turned out, was a grave mistake.

. . . . . . . . . .

Bones paced in his room trying to figure out what to do with Alice's menus—the real ones he'd taken from the box in the kitchen. In the end, he tore them up and flushed them down the toilet. Bye-bye, Brussels sprouts. Farewell, garbanzo beans. Adios, toasted rye crisps. He'd just finished the last flush when he heard Lard in the bedroom. "Hey, man," he said. "I found more CRAP."

"Yeah?"

"I'll put it on your desk," Lard said. "Back in a sec."


Calvin wondered, not for the first time, if being CRAP meant you were a little bit crazy. If allowing yourself to have feelings, like they said, was the definition of madness. "Where did you come from?" he asked the girl.

"Womb-X," she said, seemingly ashamed. She rolled onto one side, pulling her knees up, hugging them close, as if trying to disappear altogether.

Calvin stared at the curve of her back. Perfect, unflawed. He'd purr her name if he knew it.

He stepped lightly over her. She seemed confused to see him still there. "I hear there are others like us," she said in a dreamy breath. "Up here. Hiding out."

He kneeled, his neoprene against her flesh. She too had removed her auditory phone. Wires dangled dangerously from her ear. But he couldn't believe she'd disconnected her feeding tube.

"Are you hungry?" he asked.

She looked starved.

She unfolded her arms, straightening her legs. He bent down, gently inserting his tube through the slit in her uniform into her navel clamp, allowing his life juice to flow into her.

They had to get away from here.

The story was fascinating in part because it was so frightening. And it seemed a sign, albeit in a freakish way, that Bones wasn't alone. It had to do with Calvin's longing for the girl he'd just met, and like Bones and Alice, they were in the early stages of getting to know each other.

"Chu Man wants to see you in his office," Lard said, sauntering back in. "Since it's your weekly progress report, try to act like someone who's, you know, making progress."

# 18

Today Dr. Chu wore a light blue shirt and navy blue tie. It looked like a grape Popsicle had detonated in his mouth and splattered his shirt with purple juice. His face was shiny with some kind of cream that made it impossible to look at him without squinting.

He sat rigidly behind his desk thumbing through a thick file. Bones knew he was done for when Dr. Chu said, "I just finished a conference call with your parents."

Since Bones couldn't look at him directly without blinking unnaturally, he focused on the tie. "It isn't their fault that I'm in here," he said.

Dr. Chu didn't change his expression. "I told them you were making progress," he said.

Bones nodded because it seemed the appropriate thing to do. Besides, what could he say? Another fifteen minutes and the gang would be on the roof smoking it up. "My parents feel responsible for me being in here, which doesn't make me feel that great."

"Great?" Dr. Chu leaned forward, pen clicking. "Can you be more specific?"

"You know, responsible. *Guilty.*"

Bones wasn't sure when *feeling* guilty had morphed into *being* guilty. Or when he'd started believing he didn't deserve anything better. He'd hoped admitting this to himself would have made him feel better. It didn't.

Dr. Chu closed the file. "I'd like you to write your family a letter," he said. "And tell them what you just told me."

Bones stared into his lap.

"But you don't have to send it. And you don't have to show it to me—just let me know when it's finished. Fair enough?"

Bones did the nodding thing again. "Okay."

"Oh, and you should know, we've decided to increase your caloric intake…"

*(What a surprise!)*

"Gradually, to avoid unnecessary health issues…"

*(Fat is the new thin.)*

"You'll have a choice of a fat-free protein bar or a milkshake with vitamins and minerals…"

*(Death by calories.)*

"…every afternoon," Dr. Chu said.

He might as well have said, *Lean forward so I can hammer thumbtacks into your head.*

"How many calories?" Bones had to know.

Dr. Chu's mouth formed two zeros. "About one hundred."

A hundred calories equaled jogging in place twelve minutes.

. . . . . . . . . .

Bones took the stairs to the roof, bursting through the metal fire door. He sprinted over to Lard and Teresa, who were sitting on the edge of the tomato bed. Teresa's jeans were looser than ever. She was drawing a peace sign on Lard's Band-Aid.

"How'd it go with Chu Man?" Lard asked. "Did you impress him with your humility? Toss out a few agonizing emotions?"

Bones was still jogging; three minutes to go. "Something like that."

"That's my man!"

Bones glanced at the door hoping Alice would appear in a leotard and tights with a sheer skirt tied around her tiny waist, the afternoon sun casting light on her strawberry hair.

Lard lit up and stared at the fat doobie between his fingers, as if the rich smoke came from the purest crop. That's when Bones first suspected Lard was growing the stuff up here—maybe in with the tomatoes or hidden in pots behind old equipment.

Lard took another hit and gave Bones a look of mock contempt. "Just so you know, it looks like the green beans will live."

Bones ramped up the last minute. *Fifty-nine, fifty-eight,*

*fifty-seven...* Then he sagged in a chair, waiting for his pulse to return to normal.

Lard watched him rain sweat. "Don't you like ever just kick back?"

"Or want a snack?" Teresa asked. "It's okay to be nice to yourself."

*Ugh!*

To relieve the stress Lard struck a false posture of power a la Dr. Chu and his cohorts. "It's okay to act out, son," he said in a mockingly serious tone. "Since you suffer from ARRD, otherwise known as Anal Retentive Regressive Disorder."

"Constipation?" Bones joked back.

"I said anal, not anus."

Teresa adopted an expression of concern. "Tell us about your fetishes, son."

"We want to help you psycho-bitch your babble." Lard again. Then he slipped into his mellow stoned zone. "Relax, man. She'll be here."

Bones got up and jogged back across the roof. He made his way down the stairs to the dayroom where Mary-Jane and Elsie were sitting with towels draped over their shoulders. It looked like they were coloring each other's hair with tomato juice.

"Anyone seen Alice?" Bones asked.

Mary-Jane said, "No, sorry."

Elsie snipped, "She broke her leg and we had to shoot her."

She had the brain of an empty jar.

Bones stood in front of Alice's closed door. Doors were never closed. *Never.* Just then Unibrow came down the hall with a mop and bucket of cleaning supplies. "They wheeled her downstairs about an hour ago."

"Hasn't she given enough blood?" Even as Bones said it he knew that wasn't it. He backed away, a big pulse of sickness thudding through him.

"That girl is a cardiac arrest looking for a place to happen," Unibrow said. "Her heart was beating faster than the speed of sound."

Bones flew down the corridor. *Downstairs.* What did that mean? The emergency room? He rounded the corner and slammed into an orderly he'd never seen before. "Hey!" the guy said. "What's the hurry?"

Bones wasn't about to stop to answer. When he reached the elevator, he frantically punched the *down* button. *Come on!* The door opened and he squeezed into a wall of people. Seconds later the doors opened onto a polished corridor marked emergency room.

The waiting room was annoyingly sterile and notably more depressing than the EDU. Bones just stood inside looking around at people who clutched plastic numbers as if waiting in line at a bakery for a doughnut. A TV was tuned to the Shopping Network, blasting loud enough to make him think of earplugs, but it couldn't drown out the wheezing moans and fear.

He forced his feet in the direction of a chest-high window that kept the receptionist immune from bacteria. When he tapped on the glass a woman opened it from the other side. He thought she'd look more human without the hair net.

"Can I help you?" she asked.

Bones heard the whirring of life-saving machines behind her. "Alice," he said too loud.

*Crap! What was her last name?*

Bones was beyond frantic. "They brought her down a few hours ago from the EDU."

"Oh, right. They took her—" She paused to type something into her computer.

*Took her where? OR? ICU? The morgue?*

She looked up, eyes narrowing. "Are you related?"

He nodded. "Her brother."

"Yes, I see the resemblance," she said, head tilted. "She's on the sixth floor."

Bones didn't bother to ask if she could have visitors. He knew the answer, *no*. He hit the elevator and got off on the sixth floor with its impersonal hallway and infinite linoleum. He rushed blindly past a nurse's station void of nurses.

Crap, he'd forgotten to ask the receptionist for Alice's room number. He took endless turns, peeking in and out of rooms. Oxygen tents. Respirators. Tubes in arms, noses, mouths. Everyone looked scared to death.

Bones found Alice in a room with a single bed. The startling paleness of her skin, smooth and light as if she'd been swimming in mayonnaise. Yet her cheekbones were too pronounced, her skin as transparent as parchment paper. She lay smothered in blankets. Light came in through the blinds, cutting her into slats.

He stood in the doorway, wondering about the many machines. An IV ran into Alice's right arm, linking her with a bag of clear liquid. Her left arm had what looked like a blood pressure cuff. It connected to a machine with a digital screen that flashed her heart rate, blood pressure, and a number he didn't understand.

Bones watched Alice purr before he took a quiet step inside. He was so relieved at seeing her he could barely breathe. He watched the line of her heart rate rise and dip into valleys. *Beep, beep, beep.* He couldn't imagine losing her—his love, his life—after he'd just begin to live himself.

Her eyelids fluttered lightly. A finch fallen from its nest.

"Alice?" he whispered, now beside her bed.

"Bones?" Her voice was thin.

When he held her limp hand, she squeezed back. "Are you okay?" He inhaled her sweet air. "How're you feeling?"

"That depends." She smiled, her eyes still closed. "How do I look?"

"Like a delicately carved bird."

"Come closer," she whispered.

"Okay." But he couldn't get any closer without climbing over the bedrail.

"Tell me a story, Bones," she said, her eyelashes watering. "Something to take me away from here."

Bones would do anything she asked, although he was lousy when it came to telling jokes or stories. Then he thought about a kid named Calvin who wore a neoprene wetsuit and risked imprisonment to play his guitar. He told Alice what he knew about Calvin's love for a beautiful girl. How they struggled to survive after the present world was destroyed by who knew what?

Then he leaned down and kissed her forehead.

"What're you doing there?" she said, teasing him.

"Uh, I didn't want to mess up your lipstick?"

Alice smiled again, a nervous little twitch. He'd never hungered for her more.

Bones was about to tell her the rest of what he knew about CRAP when the line on the screen spiked.

"Alice?"

No answer.

*Alice?*

Nothing.

*Wake up!*

Suddenly two sumo wrestlers in nurses' uniforms stormed the room screaming medical stuff he didn't understand, although, "What the hell are you doing in here?" seemed clear enough.

Bones stepped back cringing when the biggest nurse jabbed Alice's arm with a needle. He looked back at the screen, watching the ping-pong ball that was her heartbeat. He began praying inside, barely breathing. After an eternity the line evened out, slowly at first, like a simmer.

"What's wrong with her?" He was crying now.

"I don't know who you are or what you're doing in here," the nurse spat with an accusing look. "But you have to leave."

"Alice—" He had to say her name, say good-bye.

*"Now."*

Bones breathed in Alice's air again before backing out of the room. He was in the hall just outside her door when one of the wrestlers barreled out, nearly knocking him down. "Do I have to call security?"

"I'm leaving," Bones muttered.

Then he retraced his steps back to the fourth floor.

He couldn't get his brain around what had happened to her. Just last night he'd helped her sneak off the ward to rehearse—watched her fly up and down stairs, skim the landings in pink satin, never breaking a sweat.

..........

Bones approached the dayroom slowly, surprised to hear what sounded like a meeting in progress, not even caring that he was done for if he missed one. He hugged the wall, peeking around the corner.

Lard sat on the couch next to Teresa.

"She suffered heart failure..." Nancy was saying.

Bones let out the air he'd been holding in. Alice's air. Heads turned at the sound. For a terrible moment everything was quiet; nothingness filled the space. All he could do was stare back.

*Alice.*

*They're talking about Alice.*

Bones tried to get his shoes in a forward motion, wondering where his balance had gone.

Nancy caught his eye. "She died a week before her thirty-third birthday—"

Bones didn't hear what came next. He staggered to a chair and fell into it choked by relief.

*Not Alice. Not Alice. Not Alice.*

They had to be talking about Eve.

"The coroner said she died because of heartbeat irregularities brought on by chemical imbalances," Nancy said. "They also cited cachexia—meaning extremely low weight and weakness."

Mary-Jane sat with her feet on a chair, chin on her knees. "Why couldn't her doctors do something?"

"Karen was still using laxatives," Nancy went on. "Even while she was under the care of a psychotherapist—"

*Karen?*

Bones finally got it.

They were talking about that singer from the 1970s—her story was legendary in therapy groups like this. But he knew this wasn't about Karen Carpenter. Not really. It was about Alice. That's why Nancy had called the meeting.

"Anyways," Elsie said. "I heard she gained thirty pounds in two months."

Nicole rocked in her chair. "Maybe it was the shock of her body trying to be normal that killed her."

"That's too much at one time," Teresa said. "No one's body can handle that."

"Could something like that happen to Alice?" Nicole asked.

"It's impossible to know," Nancy said.

The room grew quiet.

And suddenly Bones understood.

Alice couldn't lose anymore weight.

Not now.

Not ever.

# 19

Lard stormed around their room, his combat boots seriously attacking linoleum. His face was so red Bones thought his cheeks would burst from the pressure. *Splat*. Blood vessels all over the aggressively sterile walls. He opened his journal, took out Alice's phony menus, and threw them at Bones.

"Do you think I give a shit that you lied to me about the fucking green beans?" Anger spread like a fever down his neck. His eyes were magnified behind his glasses. "YOU ALMOST KILLED HER, DICKHEAD!"

Bones looked around helplessly, completely lost. He wanted to stop the clock, give himself a second chance to do it over again. Rewind his trip to the kitchen; bypass the box on the counter with the menus. All he could do was stare at the floor and try to picture Alice back on the ward.

"You think I don't know that you two meet every night? And exercise like sick fucks? But did I say anything about it?

148

No. None of my business, I told myself while she got skinny enough to thread through a needle."

Bones knew he did this to her.

*All by myself.*

"You were there when I refused to substitute those menus." Lard punched the air. "You heard me say it was suicide."

*I'm going to be sick.*

"I thought you cared about her, man. I thought you *loved* her."

"Stop it!" Bones ran to the bathroom.

Lard chased him, pummeling the fake wood door. "I'm not finished!"

Bones barely got his pants down, falling backward on the toilet seat, grasping at the waste can. His body erupted in a brown explosion from one end, dry heaves from the other. He flushed and flushed wishing he could go down with the mess.

The next voice he heard was Unibrow's. "What's going on in there?" he called through the door.

"Get lost!" Bones shouted back.

"Open up!"

"No!"

Bones hit the shower to scrub off the stink of panic and worry and guilt.

Lard was right.

*I could have killed her!*

Until his last meeting with Dr. Chu, Bones hadn't spent

that much time thinking about guilt. Sure he felt bad about his family. But the guilt he felt about Alice was all consuming, like a million needles injecting poison into his heart.

*Guilt.*

An invisible tattoo scarring him for life.

Lard was gone when he came out of the bathroom. Unibrow stood in his place. "Guess that door's going to have to come off its hinges."

"Bring on the screwdrivers," Bones said.

"Chu isn't going to like this," Unibrow said on his way out.

Bones didn't know what to do. He collapsed in his chair and stared at the letter he'd started to his parents. He'd gone on and on, thanking them for getting him up for school every morning, for staying a safe distance back when he went trick-or-treating. Bullshit like that.

He tore the page from his notebook, crumpled it into a ball, and flung it on the floor. None of that stuff mattered now. He stared at a new page, trying to remember when he'd started telling his friends he was allergic to pizza then eating the crust they tossed back in the box. Or standing in front of the fridge obsessing over a doggie bag brought home by his parents. Sixth grade. Maybe seventh. That was around the time he thought calories in other people's food didn't count.

His sister had been right. His sister had been right when she told him that everyone suffers damage on some level—just from being on the planet. The bigger issue was how people cope. Do they admit it, deal with it, and move on? Or numb themselves with drugs? Food? Or spend the rest of their lives shielding themselves from the Valerie Willendorfs of the world?

Bones picked up his pen and forced himself to tell his mom and dad what he was thinking, what he was feeling, really feeling, down in his gut, as honestly as he could. He started by telling them chunky kids were always chosen last for kickball, about cross-eyed Jenny Willendorf and the custard disaster, about the bitch at the department store handing him a pair of Husky jeans, wishing he'd been upfront about the impact these things had on him.

Writing a letter, knowing he didn't have to send it, helped him understand what people had been telling him for a long time—he wouldn't get better unless he worked at it. He had to want it, really want it. He was the only one who could exorcise his demons. He had to learn to do things differently.

He closed his journal and leaned back, balancing precariously on two chair legs. He knew Alice would have rehearsed with or without him. And she would have found a way to trade menus if he hadn't done it.

But none of that mattered.

Bones had thought he was helping her. But he was really helping her stay sick, because he was just as sick in his own sick way.

After a long hour of staring at nothing, Lard came in stomping heavily to his side of the room. He set his lunchbox on his desk with a thud. "In case you're interested," he said, tossing a piece of paper on his desk. "Here's more of the story. I found it in an empty Tupperware container."

"Have you heard anything about—" Bones tried.

Lard slugged the question. "Just shut the fuck up before this day gets any worse."

Bones read the page in silence.

Calvin and Lily met like this each night after curfew in the mangled milieu of colorless glass, steel, and concrete that were once museums, libraries, concert halls, and video arcades. He played his guitar while she painted, using the old-world technique of fresco. Tons of plaster littered the ground, so no problem there.

She lulled him with endearing tales of paintbrushes woven from her own silky hair and tints she mixed from bodily fluids. "I tried state sanctioned art in school," she said with a lazy stroke. "I prefer Jackson Pollock to Warhol and his soup cans. Don't you, my love?"

Calvin nodded.

"If we're going to stay together," she said, her voice no longer frail or tired, gaining strength from his nightly injections. "We can't keep meeting like this, it isn't safe. It isn't romantic."

The universe had dropped the perfect woman in his junk heap.

Now Bones knew what he'd suspected all along. George

was writing about the EDU, a place as twisted by rules and rituals as the fictional world he'd created. His Excellence was a metaphor for the supreme self-important authoritarian, Dr. Chu. Bones couldn't believe he hadn't figured it out sooner. George had been in love with Alice too. It made Bones crazy to think he might have stuck his tube in her…No, he couldn't, *wouldn't* go there.

· · · · · · · · · ·

Two days later, Lard was at his desk eating Cheese Doodles with Rachael Ray. Bones was too depressed to crack his new magazine. He bent over his journal writing the type of letter to his family that he could actually mail, telling them some of the things he'd learned in the program, explaining how he'd heard most of it before, but things were going to be different because now he'd started listening and wanted to change.

"Someone switched our room number from nineteen to sixty-nine," Lard said, grabbing his lunchbox.

"That sucks."

"Funny, *not*," Lard said. "Since I'm not attracted to you in that or any other way. *Whatsoever*."

"Three guesses who did it?"

"Elsie."

Bones nodded. "She definitely spent too much time in the birth canal."

"You think?"

Bones started to follow Lard down the hall when he

realized Lard was on his way to the kitchen. Nancy stopped Bones in the dayroom with her usual smile. "Alice is doing much better." She squeezed Bones's shoulder affectionately. "Her heart is strong and there doesn't appear to be any permanent damage to her other organs."

Bones let himself breathe.

"They're moving her from ICU into a regular room," Nancy said. "She was lucky this time, real lucky."

Luck had touched them both.

Teresa sauntered over with Mary-Jane and Elsie. Nancy answered the most basic questions. *Vital signs, stable. Mom and Dad with her. Field trip to the gift shop to buy her a get-well gift.*

Bones ate dinner alone, his back to the others. And while the skinless chicken breast on his plate didn't look all that appetizing, it didn't look entirely revolting either. He reached for the saltshaker.

"What happened to your gloves?" Elsie snipped. "Did Lard eat them?"

Bones stared at his bare fingers, struck by the sudden shock of forgetting to put them on.

After dinner, Unibrow escorted the crew downstairs to the shop. "Five minutes, max."

They crammed into a space aglow with too much optimism. Helium-filled balloons skipped overhead. *Get Well Soon!* seemed overly cheery. Bones blew dust off plastic flowers while Teresa, Mary-Jane, Sarah, and Nicole tried on jewelry. Lard flipped through cookbooks.

"Rachael Ray may be hot," he said. "But Julia Child is the bomb."

A debate broke out over which stuffed animal to buy. A floppy-eared cocker spaniel or a droopy-eyed basset hound. Bones held out for a bear with marble eyes and a crooked smile. "Perfect," Teresa said.

The clerk smoothed out their crumpled bills. "You're four dollars and sixty-eight cents short," she said.

Unibrow made up the rest. Even more surprising, everyone agreed Bones should deliver the bear. But then, he thought, miserable all over again, only Lard knew that swapping the menus had almost killed her.

. . . . . . . . . .

Bones slumped limply at his desk. The room was a tomb. Boring and utterly lonely. He didn't feel like going to the roof, not while Alice was stuck upstairs. TV applause drifted in from the dayroom. A phone rang.

Anytime he tried talking to Lard, Lard snapped, "What is it about shut-the-fuck-up you don't understand?"

It was like trying to communicate with someone onshore from a sinking ship. It was pointless, but Bones kept trying to convince Lard that he'd never hurt Alice on purpose. That he'd never do anything to hurt her, though he was completely aware of how completely and absolutely he had hurt her.

He spent the rest of the evening at his desk working on a get-well card. He tore pages from an old magazine, cut out words, and pasted them onto a sheet of construction paper he found with the art supplies. *Dance. Dream. Hope. Laugh. Get. Well. Soon.*

*Sincerely yours* and *Your friend* sounded too impersonal. He signed it *Love, Bones*. That was the truth.

The next day Nancy came in to tell him he could see Alice. "Just to deliver the bear," she said. "Make it snappy."

"Okay."

He took the elevator to the sixth floor. All this time he'd been dying to see her, and now he stood outside her door afraid to knock.

"Who's the bear for?" a nurse asked.

"For a friend," he said.

"Alice?"

Bones nodded.

She winked at him. "You go right in, sweetie."

Alice was propped up in a chair reading *Dance Magazine*. Her lips were ripe plums and her hair was brushed to one side in a sloppy braid. She was mummified in wool scarves.

She looked up and smiled when she saw him. "So there's this choreographer who asks dancers to improv during auditions. Sixty seconds, anything goes. Nothing can be wrong, I mean, technically. God it would be so scary to have to make up your own steps on the spot like that."

"You'd do great," Bones said, walking around the foot of the bed. "This is from everyone on the ward."

Her eyes sparkled. "Look at that crooked smile."

Bones handed her the card. "And this is from me."

Alice took the card, running her finger over the words. "I love it, Bones."

There was that word again.

"I'm sorry for—" His words caught, but he had to say it. "Nancy said you could have died…like that singer."

"Karen Carpenter?" she asked. "I can't believe they're still using her like that."

He didn't know what to say.

"Wait'll I tell you about this dream I had," she said. "Probably because of the meds, but still, it was like watching an indie movie."

Bones knew he'd already been there too long, but he stayed and listened while she described a love affair between two teenagers, Calvin and Lily. He was about to mention her friend from last summer, George, and explain that he'd written the story when her parents appeared in the doorway. They wore heavy make-up like they'd just come from the theater. Their eyes drawn on with thick black pencil, and their mouths formed fake smiles.

Her mom glided across the room with a bouquet of roses. "How's our little girl today?" she asked.

Alice mumbled under her breath, "God I need a cigarette."

# 20

Another page waited on Bones's desk, presumably deposited by Lard.

Luxurious nights passed while Lily ground plaster and mixed pigment in preparation for their journey. Calvin tuned his guitar to her heartbeat. The frequency both soothed and consumed him.

He picked her up on his ten-speed one exquisite night. The sky was moonless. No stars. No asteroids. Only dust particles and chemical pollutants extending without bounds into the atmosphere. He'd attached a second seat for Lily and a basket for Michelangelo.

Lily smiled when she saw him, entwining her arms snugly around his bare waist. "Put this on," he said, slipping the top half of his wetsuit over what remained of her ragged uniform. He wore the leggy part. "So you'll blend with the darkness."

"If only..." she said, then stopped.

Calvin understood completely. No one could be wholly beautiful in state-issued shoes. Guaranteed ugly for life. He waited a respectful moment and stepped from his boots. "Wear these."

Lily smiled, lovely as a cellulose rose.

Suddenly the whole world opened up to him. He wondered why the terminally ill let themselves be controlled by time and clocks, as if ancient Egyptians monitored the 24-hour cycle.

Why the diseased and dying didn't rise from beneath His Excellence's tyrannical thumb. Break into the state repository and steal bicycles, skateboards, wheelchairs—anything to ride an unbroken line away from the tyrannical dictator to freedom? What did they have to lose?

Lard came in less noisy than usual. "Why can't a person cook in the dishwasher?" he asked randomly.

Bones was so relieved Lard was talking to him, he answered too quickly. "Maybe if you took out the top rack."

Lard stared at him, eyes big as oysters behind his glasses. For a microsecond, Bones thought he'd misunderstood the question. "Cook someone in a dishwasher? Isn't that what you said? Though you'd probably go to jail."

Lard looked confused then nearly busted his wide girth of a gut. "I mean a person, like me, could use the dishwasher for cooking, instead of say, an oven, stove, or crock-pot. Think about it. Halibut crimped in foil. Timed cycles. No soap. *Steam*. It would poach in its own juices."

"Seriously?" Bones asked.

"Maybe I'll even write a cookbook some day." Lard grabbed his journal, scribbling. "Go on talk shows—tell people how I was killing myself with food. Think it would help other poor slobs like us?"

"It might."

"You know that guy George?" Bones asked, one-third because the ice wall between them was melting, and two-thirds because he had to know. "What was his diagnosis?"

"He was on the wrestling team at his school but too heavy to make weight in his division," Lard said, all without detouring from his task. "Creative guy, but thoroughly gross in his methods, if you ask me. Wore football jerseys. Liked warm beer."

"What happened to him?" Bones asked.

"I heard he quit wrestling after he left here," Lard said. "Went back to being a fun-loving, beer drinking guy. You two have a lot in common."

Lard didn't have to say it.

*Alice.*

# 21

It took Bones about thirty seconds to get ready for their next field trip, an undisclosed restaurant downtown. After a steamy hot shower he put on clean sweats, and leaned into the mirror to pick a piece of lint from his head. Maybe he'd let his buzz grow out. Lard tried to tame his mane with hair goop.

Mary-Jane and Elsie looked like they had coffee stains around their eyes. Some sort of grunge makeup. Their hair was this weird orange color. Tomato juice. Elsie wore cowboy boots and her usual cut-offs. Her shorts were so skimpy the pockets hung out the bottoms like tongues. A T-shirt fell off one shoulder, *Feed My Lips*.

Nancy escorted everyone downstairs.

Sarah wore her sunglasses the normal way, chattering incessantly with Nicole about abdominal bloating. It had taken Bones a while to figure out Sarah. One day she refused salt or caffeine due to migraines. The next day, no gluten. Chronic fatigue. Today she complained of being lactose intolerant. Here was the thing, Sarah wasn't faking. It was more like some kind of food hypochondria.

A van pulled up in front of the main lobby. Dr. Chu controlled the wheel, sporting a casual golf shirt sans tie. Lard called shotgun.

"Buckle up," Dr. Chu ordered after they settled in.

They clicked their seatbelts.

The sky was dark and foggy, like clinical depression. Bones hated that Alice wasn't with them and worried constantly that her parents would check her out of the program as soon as she was strong enough. They were take-charge kind of people, that was obvious.

Dr. Chu drove a couple of miles down a two-lane boulevard over newly painted crosswalks, passing endless strip malls. Half-dead palm trees busted sidewalks with their roots. Billboards advertised used car lots. Fluorescent tubes on liquor store windows touted Lotto tickets.

There was an abundance of hot-looking girls with flesh screaming between layers of spandex. A fat mother yanked two fat kids down the pavement. In spite of the heat, a homeless guy wore a miner's helmet and heavy jacket covered with pennies. A scrawny dog tagged behind him. Typical Los Angeles.

Dr. Chu lectured them via the rearview mirror. "Feel free to ask the waitstaff questions." He'd cranked the AC to keep their nerves in check. "But make an effort to keep them within the bounds of propriety."

Bones tried and failed to ignore the endless string of ethnic restaurants, all with the same smoky glass fronts. He slid lower in the seat but they taunted him. Chinese. Japanese. Korean. Filipino. Thai. Vietnamese.

Twenty minutes later, Dr. Chu was ushering them to a long table in a restaurant called Mustache Pete's. Bones couldn't believe he'd picked a place with hair in its name. He wasn't sure if the dining room really smelled like sauerkraut or if he'd been in the hospital too long.

They chose up sides of the table and read menus uncertainly. Teresa picked at her nails. Even Lard looked uneasy. He blinked too fast. Bones had a nervous urge to use the bathroom—like now—and since he hadn't eaten since breakfast, meaning there wasn't anything to throw up, Dr. Chu said he could go alone.

"Five minutes," Dr. Chu said, a wary eyebrow rising. "Then I'm sending in the troops."

Bones stood up and sucked in his gut, squeezing by a table of women in suits, maneuvering toward a lit bathroom sign. A payphone hung on the wall in a corridor between *His* and *Hers*. He looked over his shoulder to make sure he couldn't be seen, then slid quarters into the slot and dialed his sister's cell.

"Are you okay?" she asked as soon as she heard his voice.

Bones heard Pink Floyd in the background and pictured her sprawled on her comforter, World Peas travel mug in hand. "Just missing you guys," he answered.

"I miss you too," she said easily. "I thought it was against hospital rules to call home."

"I'm at a payphone in a restaurant."

"Restaurant?"

"A field trip, but don't worry. I'll live through it."

Dishes clanked and a blood-curdling cry radiated from the direction of the kitchen. Bones peeked around the corner. Apparently everyone at his table had heard the sound as if puppies were being slaughtered.

"How're mom and dad?" he asked, turning back to the phone.

"Mom's still doing a lot of reading about, you know—"

"Anorexia?"

Jill suddenly got quiet. "I'm not used to hearing you say it."

Bones got quiet too. "How's Dad?"

"Busier than usual." Her voice smothered him in a hug. "We got your letter yesterday. God, Jack, I wish you would've told us about that stuff before. Little kids can be such pricks."

"Yeah."

"I was Jill the Sour Dill in kindergarten," she said. "The damage isn't too deep."

"I'd better go, sis. Love you."

"Love you too, weirdo," which wasn't a bad thing to hear.

. . . . . . . . . .

The color of his pee had gone from root beer when he'd first checked in to the program to herbal tea. Now it was as light as fresh squeezed lemonade. Bones washed his hands vigorously and used a paper towel to open the bathroom door.

The middle of the table had grown condiments since he'd left. Catsup (1 tablespoon, 12 calories), mustard (1 teaspoon, 3 calories), pickle relish (1 tablespoon, 20 calories). Some with zero calories: hot sauce, salt, pepper.

Nadine, their server, wore a bolo tie and a plaid blouse that looked like packets of sugar had been sewn into it. She made everything sound like a question, as if she was apologizing. Bones half expected her to throw in a y'all.

"To get you started?" She set down two plates of raw vegetables. "Take a few more minutes?"

"Have some celery," Lard said to Bones. "Dr. Chu will go easier on you if you eat something on your own."

*I can do this.*

*No, you can't.*

*Yes, I really can.*

Bones felt an odd mix of old fears and new ones as he reached for a celery stick. He used his bread plate to make a paste with salt and water. He looked up catching the table's stare. "*What?*"

"Nothing."

"It's okay."

"Don't worry about it."

Bones had been in the hospital a little more than two weeks with less than four to go. Meals were still such a bitch, like listening to Jay-Z on helium. He knew that was what the field trip was about—to see how everyone handled food in the real world.

Bones studied his menu, trying to ignore the crunch of something, well, crunchy on the floor under his shoes. What tripped him up most was that he didn't know all the ingredients, and therefore the calories, in sauces, gravies, marinades, dressings.

His old friend panic returned to poke his eyeballs with a fork. A glass shattered behind him. Someone swore.

Nadine came back to the table tapping her pen on a tablet.

"Have you decided, Jack?" Dr. Chu asked.

Bones couldn't believe he wanted to start with him. He snapped the celery stick in half. Nadine jumped like she'd been shot. "House salad. Dressing on the side." He mumbled into his chin while running a piece of celery through the salt bath. "No tomatoes, cucumbers, cheese, or croutons."

Nadine looked perplexed. "Just lettuce?"

"Welcome to the world of Holy Cabbage," Lard said. "Lettuce pray."

Bones licked salt off his celery. "And a glass of water, please. A lemon slice if it's not cut too thick."

Nicole unhooked the rubber bands from her braces. "Me too."

"Same here," Sarah and Mary-Jane said.

It was Lard's turn to order. "I'll have the grilled turkey burger and fries."

"Sounds good to me," Teresa said.

"Uh, wait a sec," Lard interrupted himself. "How often do you change the oil in the fryer?"

"Once a week?" Nadine said, absently checking her apron, as if looking for a spare pen.

"What day?" he asked.

"This morning?" she said.

"Corn oil?"

"Yes, sir?"

"Doesn't your cook know corn oil is high in poly-unsaturated fats and goes through oxidation more readily than other oils—" Lard was so loud that people turned from their tables to listen. "If it's okay, I'll substitute sliced tomatoes for fries."

Nadine nodded, only too eager to move on to Elsie, who asked if she could order Chocolate Decadence Cheesecake as an entrée. The answer was resounding silence while Dr. Chu clasped his hands so tight his knuckles pulsed white.

"Scratch that. I'll have lasagna with extra meat sauce," Elsie said. "A side order of flour tortillas and diet soda. Large."

Nancy ordered grilled fish.

Dr. Chu chose a BLT. "And bring a platter of sliced turkey breast, low-fat cottage cheese, and hard-boiled eggs."

For the salads.

Dessert wound up being a forty-five minute meeting back at the hospital to discuss the outing. The girls seemed okay with the experience and suggested it as a weekly activity. Bones said he thought he would have been less anxious if he could have seen a menu ahead of time.

Elsie said that was dumb. "That isn't how it'll be when we get out of here."

Lard was quick to point out that better restaurants had websites and posted their menus. "That's how people who care about what they eat decide where they want to go."

Score one for the beta males.

All of a sudden Bones was aware of gas gurgling in his stomach. *From the cottage cheese and hard-boiled eggs!* He rushed down the hall to his room, pressing his hands into his gut to keep it from expanding.

# 22

Bones didn't remember falling asleep that night but then he never remembered. He woke up worn out from the field trip and his first day in the exercise room. Normally he would've been ecstatic to spend twenty minutes jogging between a Sunny Health Fitness Indoor Cycling Bike and Anti-Burst Gym Ball. But Unibrow stuck to him like stink. The guy must have lived on raw garlic.

He rolled over and clutched his pillow to his chest. In his drowsy state he wondered if anyone would notice if he slept through breakfast. Yeah, right. He forced himself up on one elbow, and squinted at Lard, who was at his desk with his girls: Rachael, Julia, and Martha. Giada had recently joined the harem.

Bones yawned. "What time is it?"

"I need another way to cook SPAM," Lard said. "Or shoot myself in the foot."

"You're kidding, right?"

Lard disappeared into the bathroom. From the sounds emanating through the doorway, the cubicle would need fumigating before Bones could go in there.

"That's what I call a dump," came Lard's voice with a flush. He surfaced tying the drawstrings on his pants. "If I was as crazy as you are, I'd weigh it."

Bones was turning his socks inside out so he could get another day out of them. "Feces is fifty percent water," he said.

Lard grunted. "Only you would know that."

"I didn't get this way by not knowing a thing or two about a thing or two."

"Ya think?"

"Try a garnish," Bones said. "Just tie a scallion around it or something."

"Sometimes you scare me, man."

"I'm talking about SPAM, you idiot, not the turd."

Lard groaned. "And *I'm* talking about you're crazy. You don't have to tackle everything at once. Just start with one or two things, like losing the gloves. That was a start."

The scary thing was Bones knew what Lard meant. They were turning into an old married couple, reading each other's minds and finishing each other's sentences. Bones wondered when they'd start to look alike. Not a happy thought.

"And you're definitely less obsessed with calisthenics than you were when you first got here." Lard said. "You made it through lunch at the restaurant without having a heart attack. So technically, that's three things."

That didn't make Bones feel better.

It made him feel fat.

· · · · · · · · · ·

When Alice moved back to the ward, things quickly returned to normal, meaning Alice, Bones, Lard, and Teresa hung out during meals, between meetings, and after writing assignments.

Alice had recovered faster than any of her doctors had thought, notably because she'd had such close supervision. She couldn't exercise in ICU without a nurse ratting her out, and it was nearly impossible to get rid of food. She'd been pumped with electrolyte solutions, vitamins, nutritional supplements, and who knew what else.

Alice sat down next to Bones at the lunch table, looking healthy and radiant in her black leotard. Instead of translucent skin her cheeks had a peachy blush. She wore her diamond studs, like the first time he'd seen her. A scarf hung in a way that caressed her beautiful breasts. They were fuller, plumper. Rumors about malnutrition, acute kidney failure, and shrinking heart muscle were nothing but strategy to exploit fear.

Dr. Chu delivered her lunch tray himself. "Vegetable soup and a fruit salad," he said.

Alice stared at her tray like she was reading tea leaves— calculating all two-hundred-and-fifty calories. Then she counted her vitamins. "I'm only supposed to get supplements once a day."

"It's great to have you back," Dr. Chu said before returning to the cart for another tray.

Alice covered a bored yawn. "I'm up to eighty-two pounds."

Bones wanted to tell her how beautiful she looked. Healthier. Stronger. As indestructible as hospital biscuits. Vitamins, he wanted to say, don't have many calories.

"As I see it, most of the world is just getting by—but that isn't good enough for a dancer." She pulverized a grape with the bowl of her spoon. "You have to work hard all the time. Never hold anything back."

She paused taking in Bones's star-struck gaze. It had been an agonizing five days without her. "What's the worst that can happen? You fall down. Big flippin' deal. You know what's worse?"

Bones shook his head.

"Not giving it everything you have." She glanced around, ready to swipe the grape-encrusted spoon in her napkin. "That's worse than giving up."

Dr. Chu suddenly reappeared. "May I join you?"́

Alice muttered, "*Piqué.*"

"I beg your pardon?" he asked.

Bones smirked.

She'd called him a prick.

Dr. Chu sat with them through every agonizing bite until

nothing was left but shredded napkins. Then he straightened his Mickey Mouse tie and excused himself.

"You know what I use my journal for?" Alice asked.

Bones tried to think of a clever answer but failed. "What?'

"To remind myself who I really am. Because Chu Man has some bizarre power to rewire our brains and personalities, transforming us into someone even our best friends wouldn't recognize."

It didn't seem that farfetched.

"You know what I did upstairs to keep from going insane?"

Bones was afraid to ask. "No."

"I used the sheet as a stage letting my fingers form steps in a ballet called *Giselle*. It's about a peasant girl who falls in love with a nobleman." Alice found his calf under the table with her bare foot and began rubbing tingling little circles. "It gave me an idea for a new exercise routine, but I need—"

"I can't, Alice," he said and pulled his leg away from her foot. "I mean, you could've died."

"You don't love me anymore, do you?" she said, pretending to pout. "It's because I've go*tten fat.*"

*Fat* hung in the air above their table.

It was the last thing she said to him for a very long time.

# 23

Alice had spent five days on the sixth floor at the mercy of sadistic nurses armed with syringes. Rumor had it that she had multiple transfusions to replace all the vials of blood they'd drawn. As if that even made sense.

Missing Alice and knowing he'd been responsible for her being so sick was agony. But having Alice back on the EDU and not speaking to him, was akin to drowning in a vat of chocolate syrup. She ate by herself, avoiding eye contact, and, other than therapy sessions, Bones rarely saw her. He assumed she was in her room practicing for auditions.

Lard kept saying, "She's moody, man. But don't worry, it never lasts."

Bones kept asking, "How long?"

"It isn't like she plays by the same rules as anyone else," Lard said.

Life was cruel and unfair.

On day two of the silent treatment—twenty-two-hours-

and-fifty-three minutes worth—Bones gathered the CRAP pages and slid them under Alice's door. Later that afternoon, Lard shuffled in from his shift in the kitchen. "Dinner's prepped," he said. "Let's hit the roof."

It was one of those days when the sky looked close enough to touch. Just reach up and scoop a handful of clear blue space. Bones made his way around all the junk in practiced steps and then saw Alice relaxing on her yoga mat, legs crossed at the ankles. Her eyes were closed, her face lifted to the sacred sun.

From where Bones stood he could see the freckles on her nose. He could meditate on those freckles. She wore a sheer blouse that slid off one shoulder. His eyes drew a line from the curve of her long neck to her sculpted back. A peasant skirt was hiked up showing off her milky white legs.

Lard shoved by him. "I told you she'd get over it."

Alice stirred, showing the secret hollow of her inner thigh. "Where've you been?" she asked, squinting up at them.

Bones could barely talk. "Uh, hi."

"Hi yourself."

Alice fished a cigarette and matches from her silver case, and he hurried over to light it for her. She smiled at him, inhaled, and blew out a thin stream of smoke. They were silent for a few minutes.

"I didn't know you were a writer," she finally said.

"Writer?"

"The story you slipped under my door."

Then he got it. Alice thought he'd written down what she'd told him about Calvin and Lily. A forthright person would have explained that he'd found the pages, not written them. But he couldn't resist an opportunity to impress her. "The plot was so interesting I decided to mess around with it," he said. "Expand it a bit."

Then he shrugged, all humble like.

"No really," she said. "I think it's great."

Meanwhile, Lard was digging frantically in the tomato bed for his stash. "So *not* funny, Alice."

"What am I being accused of now?" she asked.

Lard snarled at her. "What'd you do with it?"

"Maybe you hid it somewhere else?" Bones suggested. "In with the zucchini or peppers?"

Lard sat back with a groan and wiped dirt from his hands. "Gumbo," he said wearily. "I should've been more careful."

"He wouldn't rat you out, would he?" Bones asked.

"Nah, he probably just flushed it down the john."

Alice cocked her head mischievously. Her legs were still stretched out, inviting the sun to dance on her silky skin. "Listen up," she said. "I have a simple proposal. You are required to hear me out and are forbidden to say *no*."

Lard started to say something but she waved him quiet with her cigarette. "It involves a surprise party—"

"You can't surprise yourself," Lard said irritably.

"Why not? And stop interrupting me. It makes you seem like an impatient jerk that can't wait for me to finish my thoughts."

Then she sniffed, just the right effect.

As the plan unfolded, Lard began to chuckle, even though it involved breaking more rules than they could count. The most serious infraction being leaving hospital grounds without permission. Further details included Lard's '98 Celica as the getaway car.

She wasn't kidding.

*Whoa.*

"I won't survive another day in here," she said, lolling sideways. "Not without having a little fun."

Bones thought this was an entirely bad idea, but he also knew he had to go along with it to keep an eye on her. A little fun wouldn't hurt him either.

Lard decided to go with the plan, because (1) he was depressed about losing his dope, (2) Alice was intent on taking his car, and (3) going on a road trip was the least of the more serious infractions she'd offered up.

"You don't have to worry about getting caught," she said. "I've got everything figured out. And Lard? Try to look presentable."

The rendezvous time (2:45 p.m.) was right after GT, which gave them three hours before dinner, the time usually designated for assignments. The meeting place was the same for each of them: hospital parking structure.

Alice's excitement was infectious.

How could Bones say no?

# 24

Alice got to the parking lot first. She was sitting on the trunk of the ancient Celica, which was the color of a Cheese Doodle left in the sun too long. Toyota didn't even make these babies anymore.

She looked so different like this, so intensely sexy and beautiful and wonderful, Bones felt shy all over again. She had on a loose skirt and a low-cut black sweater. Her hair was pulled into a ponytail. She wore dark eyeliner and pale lipgloss.

"You look amazing," he said, knowing they'd never get away with this.

Alice re-crossed her legs working her prowess as a cock-teaser.

Bones wondered if she wore panties under her skirt. And what color they were. Black, he decided, and lacy. Probably a thong. Out of necessity he changed his focus to the Mercedes ornament on the Celica's hood. *Classy.*

Lard showed up, sweaty and stressed out. But his jeans and T-shirt were stain-free. "Let's get out of here before someone sees us."

Alice held out her hand for the keys. "Can I drive?"

"No way," Lard said.

"I have a license," she said.

"Since when?"

"Last month."

"Liar."

Lard unlocked the door, crammed in behind the wheel, and scooted the seat back. He reached across the cracked vinyl to open the passenger side. "Come on, you two delinquents. Let's make tracks!"

Bones folded himself under the low ceiling in the backseat. Not easy since he had to wade through squashed energy drink cans, an empty Bud Light bottle, and a litterbag with the governor's face on it. Aside from all the trash, the car's interior was trash.

He pushed a smelly sack of potatoes off the seat. "You making vodka back here?"

"What happens in the Doodle stays in the Doodle," Lard said and tossed his keys over his shoulder in a low arc. "Stash the spuds in the trunk."

Bones squeezed out on Lard's side with the rotten potatoes and opened the trunk. "Did you know your tags are expired?" he hollered.

"Just hurry up!" Lard hollered back.

"We can get pulled over for that," Bones said.

Lard stuck his head out the open window. "Was this my idea?"

"Just don't speed or run any lights or hit any pedestrians," Alice's voice filtered out.

Bones peered into the dark cavern of the trunk. Beside a greasy toolbox was a case of Cheese Doodles. Lard's stash, cheaper by the dozen. And randomly weird stuff like a Snoopy umbrella, Coleman stove, industrial flashlight, cracked cookie jar.

Lard pressed himself against the steering wheel, letting Bones twist back in. Seconds later the Doodle sputtered, sputtered some more, coughed oily smoke, and rumbled to life.

Five minutes later they were driving on a wide boulevard with the windows down, passing the same strip malls and tacky restaurants as on their field trip. Lard drove with two fingers on the wheel. He pushed a CD into the player and punched the button to a different track.

Mick Jagger's raspy voice crackled through the speakers. "Brown Sugar." It was cranked so loud the hula girl on the dashboard lost her lei. Lard found a roach in his ashtray and siphoned it for all it was worth. Alice fumbled a cigarette from her case and lit it, incapable of embarking on any adventure without nicotine between her slim fingers.

Lard drove and smoked.

Alice sang and smoked.

They were sailing down the San Diego Freeway, the skyline of downtown loomed twenty miles to the east. The Getty Museum rose on a weedy bluff above them to the right. The sights faded behind them as they veered onto the Santa Monica Freeway, inhaling cigarette smoke and salt-infused air.

Bones had almost forgotten what it felt like to be in the real world, driving on the four-lane freeway with cars all around. *No way we'll get away with this!* he thought. *Dr. Chu is going to eat us alive.*

Alice rummaged through the glove compartment, retrieving a package of condoms. "Afternoon Delight? *Ribbed*?"

Lard fought to grab his latex treasure. Alice won, as usual. Then, suddenly, he glanced around like he'd lost something equally important. "Crap! We forgot Teresa!"

Bones couldn't believe it either.

Lard looked doomed. "Man, oh, man."

Bones knew she probably wouldn't have come. Though he knew that wasn't the point. "She probably wouldn't have come," he said anyway.

Lard slammed his brakes at the bottom of an off-ramp— barely making a stop sign—inflicting whiplash times three. "We should've asked her," he said, strangling the steering wheel. "*I* should've asked her."

Alice ignored him, back in the glove compartment. She unearthed a wilted paperback. "*How to Shit in the Woods: An Environmentally Sound Approach to a Lost Art*?"

"For your edification," Lard said, "it's sold more than a million copies."

"If a man farts in the woods and no one's around to hear it, does he have to say *excuse me*?" she asked.

"Mine comes out in a vacuum-sealed baggy," Lard responded.

She smiled at him. "And I suppose it doesn't stink."

"You're getting my drift," he shot back.

They busted up in a way of togetherness that made Bones feel left out.

Bones wished he smoked.

Alice unbuckled her seatbelt, turned around to face him, and rested her chin on the seat. Bones wanted to lean forward and set his chin on the seat next to her. She smiled at him, her eyes stars in heaven. Bright and intensely vivid. He felt her words before she said them. "Don't ever forget this moment, promise?"

"You're going to break my heart, aren't you?" he asked.

She smiled at him again; he believed her smile.

# 25

Lard barely made the next corner, honking at a seagull dragging a half-eaten hamburger in its beak. Bones was beginning to wonder if Lard had found his license in a box of Cracker Jacks.

Alice sounded like a navigation system amped on espresso. "Turn right at the gas station! Left at the liquor store! No, the other liquor store!"

Lard swerved into a lot and parked in front a hotel that looked more like the mansions Bones had seen on Playboy TV. He imagined businessmen in their rooms mixing cocktails and doing kinky things while watching Pay-Per-View.

Bones unfolded himself from the backseat, grateful to have survived Lard's driving and daring to hope Alice had reserved them a room. Maybe even a suite. Lard must've been thinking the same thing because he said, "Isn't three a crowd?"

Alice smiled and lit another cigarette, leading them

purposefully down a stone walkway that bypassed the lobby and wrapped around a heart-shaped swimming pool. Two women sat on the steps, half immersed in water. They laughed beneath floppy hats. Another building rose on the far side of the pool. Pink flowers vined up the walls. Birds sang. Bees buzzed.

Alice stopped in front a building with a pair of etched glass doors. *Guests Only.*

"Don't look so guilty," she said and snuffed her smoke, pocketing the butt. "Haven't you ever crashed a happy hour?"

Bones and Lard traded looks. "Uh, no."

"Just pretend you're a guest." She wasn't kidding. "Come on."

They followed her into a large room—a combination living room/den/dining room. The paneled walls gleamed in highly polished wood. Couches and chairs looked cushy enough to wade in. Books with leather binding and gilded titles lined the shelves.

People, presumably those who'd paid to stay at Ocean View Suites, milled around in business suits or shorts, tank tops, and flip-flops. Alice chose a faux suede couch by the fireplace where fake logs spit real flames. "Red wine or white?" she asked.

Lard didn't hesitate. "Red."

Bones tried to shrink into himself, even though he thought he fit in okay. "What if someone wants to see our room key?"

"They never have before," she said.

"Okay, I'll try white."

The reasons Bones didn't drink alcohol were obvious — wasted calories, he wasn't much of a risk-taker, and he didn't like losing control. He dropped onto the couch next to Lard, while Alice sauntered off toward a five-star buffet table. She didn't just look like she belonged there; she looked like she owned the place and everyone in it.

Bones craned sideways, watching as she reached for a bottle of red wine. She poured confidently, carrying on a conversation with an older couple in matching terry cloth robes. Neither seemed to question her age or whether or not she was a paid guest.

Back at the couch, Alice squeezed between Bones and Lard. "To the best friends I've ever had," she said, raising her glass.

They clinked, and because Alice and Lard took sips, Bones did too. The wine wasn't as bad as he'd expected, sort of like diluted juice.

"You're a-peein'," she said wistfully.

Bones nearly choked. "*Huh*?"

"The wine," she said. "It's European."

They sank lower on the couch, convulsing in laughter.

Bones took sip after sip. It tickled his brain.

Everyone in the room was in full party mode.

Eating, drinking, storytelling, backslapping.

Lard mumbled to himself. "Teresa would love this." Then with a display of generosity he got up. "I'll get this round."

Alice scooted closer to Bones and tilted her head, asking him, "You know what's worse than letting other people run your life?"

He presumed she meant parents, teachers, therapists. But he didn't move—just shivered when she breathed on his neck, dizzy with longing and lust. She was quiet a moment, as if intense concentration was required before sharing the only secret in the universe. "Absolutely nothing," she said.

Bones nodded, and like most guys in this situation, he tried to look both thoughtful and intelligent.

"Tell me a secret, Bones," she said, blowing in his ear. "Something no one else knows."

*I love you.*

But that wasn't a secret.

*I'm a virgin.*

She probably knew that too.

He shrugged, tried to look away.

The problem with being a guy is that guys bring all of their insecurities with them wherever they go—especially into a place like this—even while sitting beside an incredibly hot anorexic girl.

He screwed up his courage to say, "I wasn't the only one worried about you—we all were. Lard and Teresa, the others."

She punched him in the arm hard. "Silly."

He frowned. "I had a dream that we were in bed together—but, you know, not like that. Just holding you."

All five quarts of blood in his body pooled in his cheeks. "Corny, huh?"

Then a guy with a hotel logo on his shirt walked around the side of the couch. Bones tried not to look guilty hoping he wasn't about to ask for a room number or ID.

"The chef is shucking oysters," the guy said. "If you'd like to try some?"

Alice smiled up at him. "Sorry, but I'm allergic."

"You, sir?"

Bones shook his head. "No thanks."

The guy moved on to the next couple.

Alice scanned the room, like she couldn't remember what they had been talking about. "Let's see if they set out anything more interesting than meatballs and cocktail wieners."

It wasn't just the mention of wieners on her tongue, but when Bones got up he had to make a quick adjustment to his pants. Alice smiled, enjoying his anguish, and strangely enough, he felt better knowing she knew.

He tagged along after her to a table that looked like a dinner party on E! Crystal platters and copper chaffing dishes. The plates were plain white china, like his mom's, but with gold edges. The silverware looked like, well, silver. He agonized over a platter of raw vegetables for a shamefully long time, silently arguing with a radish about its calories.

Then, because it was free—and because Bones knew he wouldn't have to eat it all—he took one of every vegetable just to see what his plate would look like.

Alice licked her lips. Bones wished he could do that for her. "Too bad they don't have something more original," she said. "Like hearts of palm or souls of celery."

"Peanut M&M's," Bones added. "Red."

She took a saucer, spooned Dijon mustard onto it, and glanced around the table. Bones knew she was looking for a saltshaker. He passed one to her. She smiled and shook and shook until the mustard had a layer of white.

Alice didn't really dip a celery stick into it—more like she turned it into a backhoe and shoveled in mustard. "God," she said, slightly swaying. "I've so missed this."

Lard lumbered over with a plate that looked like it had been attacked by a bear after hibernation. "I went to the kitchen to talk to the chef," he said, sucking the life out of a green olive. "After my second helping."

Alice grinned. "Thirds."

"Fine, be that way." Lard pushed his glasses up but they slid down his nose again. Bones had once seen him adjust them with a corkscrew.

"What a cool gig," Lard said. "When he's done here he goes home and plays with his kids while his wife fixes dinner."

"You'd be great at a job like this," Alice said.

They returned to the couch, joking and telling stories.

The sun coming through the high windows and the wine were mellowing them out. Alice and Bones had another glass for the road. It was quite clear that they were getting quite drunk. They quite liked it.

Lard laughed.

"What's so funny?" Alice asked, playing with a book of hotel matches.

"I never thought I'd be such good friends with a couple of reluctant eaters."

"And I never thought I'd have a friend named Lard," Bones put in.

Alice agreed it deviated from the norm.

Lard sipped coffee. "Indonesian beans."

At five fifteen they had to head back.

Cars tunneled through the fog-drift in the fading afternoon. Lard swore when they hit the freeway. Traffic was frozen on the Santa Monica East. Rush hour hadn't been part of the itinerary. A frown played on his face. "Do we have a back-up plan?"

"Yeah," Alice said, averting his gaze.

That could mean many things.

"Are you going to tell us?" Lard asked.

"Only if necessary."

Bones should have been more worried about the as-yet undisclosed strategy for sneaking back into the hospital. But there wasn't one thing he'd regret about this day—not if Dr. Chu locked him in a freezer with a hundred chicken potpies.

Alice breathed the car full of smoke while Lard changed lanes erratically and kept checking his mirrors. She put her feet on the dashboard, tucked her skirt between her knees, and started rubbing Ben Gay into her ankle. Two blocks from the hospital she motioned toward the drugstore.

The light turned red and Lard stomped on the brake. "Now?"

"Do I have to spell it out?" she said. "T-A-M-P-A-X."

"Okay. Okay." He pulled up to the curb and left the motor running.

Alice was in and out within five minutes.

Lard shifted into reverse and was backing out before she'd closed the car door. The 135-hp engine whined to life when they hit the street. The sky was fractures of orange sherbet and ripe watermelon as they cut through the hospital parking lot.

Alice tossed a box of Breathe Right Nasal Strips to Lard. "A present," she said. "For everyone on the ward."

"Gee thanks."

She reached into the sack and pulled out a bag of M&M's. "For you, Bones."

"You've been paying attention," he said.

Alice grinned at him, but he thought he saw sadness behind it. He opened the bag, picked out the red ones, and put them in his pocket. He left the rest on the seat.

Alice rolled up her window and cranked the heater. Then she opened a carton of chocolate Ex-Lax and set the foil-wrapped squares on top of the vent to melt. "I got a little something for myself too," she said.

"What the hell is that?" Lard asked, eyes alert for a parking spot.

"I'm not going to use it, I swear. It's just...insurance."

Lard was totally pissed. *"Are you kidding me?"* he said, punching the gas.

"Just because your shit doesn't stink doesn't give you the right to be an asshole," she said.

Bones slumped, stressed out all over again. It struck him that Alice probably hadn't bought any feminine hygiene products at all. She flipped the packet over the heating vent, and plucked a dance magazine and small makeup brush from the bag.

Silence nibbled at the smoky air trapped in the car. Alice used the brush to paint pages of the magazine with the melted Ex-Lax to sneak the laxatives into the hospital. She hummed *you can't always get what you want*. The pages were soon chocolate brown.

Lard watched the whole scene, gripping the steering wheel so hard his fingers looked like swollen string cheese. He eased the Doodle into an empty spot in front of the hospital and honked the horn for no reason.

"Did you have to do that?" Bones asked.

Lard honked again. "Yeah."

Bones stared at the stark white structure of the hospital, half expecting to see helicopters hovering, searchlights roaming, and a battalion of hospital police. Dr. Chu would be at the helm with an AK-47 and self-help bible.

Lard shouldered his door so hard it nearly flew off its hinges. He got out and headed across the lot without saying anything, lumbering sideways like he was playing football in slow motion.

Bones figured Lard would go to the kitchen to finish whatever he was supposed to have been doing. Gumbo had agreed to cover for him when he heard their outing involved culinary research.

Bones hurried to open Alice's door. She got out in that way girls do, like their knees are fused together. Clutching the bag, she set off for the hospital with her magazine and its laxative-coated pages.

Bones wasn't sure if he was supposed to follow her or what.

But of course he did…

# 26

A questionable looking sign hung on the elevator in a part of the hospital Bones hadn't been in before, down a long corridor in a wing opposite the emergency room. *Out of Order. Please Use Stairs.* Not surprisingly the sign was stuck on with the same type of adhesive tape Alice used on her toes.

"I didn't think we should take a chance with the stairs," she said.

Bones nodded, his buzz fading.

She punched the call button and led him into an elevator long enough for a gurney. The doors closed, sealing them inside. It was uncomfortably muggy. Somewhere between L and 4 she pressed Stop.

Bones was confused, but Alice seemed to have a purpose.

She let the bag from the drugstore drop. It hit the floor with a thud, obviously holding more than a laxative-coated magazine. Alice moved closer to him, like she didn't want the stainless steel walls to hear what she had to say.

They faced each other under the bright fluorescent light. It was so quiet he could hear his heartbeat. Then she reached out and touched his cheek, a soft tentative touch, and the world took a breath.

"Give me your hand," she said, barely a whisper.

Bones held out his hand tentatively. She took it and placed it on her heart over her left breast. So small. So delicate. She didn't move. He didn't move. Alice was his life. How could he make her his eternal?

"Kiss me," she said.

Bones let his hand linger, and then slowly slip away, not wanting her to think he was greedy. He touched her cheek, careful not to poke her in the eye. He wasn't sure what to do with his other hand, so he put it in his pocket. *Classic move.*

He felt stupid for worrying about his breath, knowing it was gross from the wine—and he worried Alice was about find out how little he knew about kissing—and he wondered if she had condoms in the bag—and imagined himself unrolling one, all suave-like—and realized he was wasting the most amazing moment in his life—and wished his brain would just shut the fuck up.

Alice leaned forward. "*Now.*"

Bones shuddered. "Okay."

He made small movements, taking her face in his hands like he'd seen in movies. He kissed the tip of her nose. He brushed his lips against hers, soft little butterfly kisses. Her lips were smooth and succulent. He closed his eyes, drinking in her essence. Cigarette smoke and wine and promise.

She touched his tongue with hers, and they were kissing, really kissing. Then somehow her tongue was probing his ear and his fingers moved to the slender curve of her waist.

"Kiss my neck. No, here. Harder. *Yes*." Alice purred. "It's okay to use your teeth."

Bones nibbled.

Alice purred louder. "*Ummm*."

Neither of them wanted to pull away.

His hand drifted slowly to her breast. This time she pressed into it. His fingers roamed to her other breast, while she traced the side of his neck with her tongue. He'd never felt anything like this. No words could describe it.

Her hand roamed down, down, down.

His heart beat fast, fast, fast.

And so loud he thought his ears would explode.

Then she touched him there.

*God.*

She began rubbing circles though his sweat pants and boxers. Softly. More circles. Then squeezing him. Gently, but firmly. Her hand wrapped around him. Steady tugs. Bones wouldn't last another second like this. He hummed inside, little explosions of ecstasy, while he lost his innocence in a six-by-eight-foot compartment that wasn't going up or down.

Alice must have leaned against the control panel, because suddenly the elevator lurched, and they stumbled off balance.

"If you get caught tell Chu Man you were outside looking for me," she said when the doors opened.

Bones squinted, light flooding in. It was too stark. Too real.

"Tell him I was out front smoking," she said. "And that I collapsed in the stairwell sneaking back in. Tell him they took me to the ER."

Alice wrapped her arms around his neck and kissed him full on the mouth—all tongue and wet warmth. "But give me a twenty-minute head start, okay?" she said, pulling back slightly.

All he could do was nod in utter bliss and stickiness.

*I love you.*

*I love you.*

*I love you.*

# 27

Bones found his way to the stairwell he usually used this time of day when sneaking back in from the roof. It was deserted as always. But it felt good to be alone with all that had just happened. He took each tread one at a time, not caring about how few calories he was burning.

For the first time in eons, he was truly happy—a happiness that swallowed him from his toes to his buzzed head. There was something about the rush of feelings when he'd kissed Alice and she'd kissed him back and her touching him in a way no one ever had. It all seemed so *right*, like everything real and honest.

. . . . . . . . . .

Bones opened the door to the fourth floor and scoured the ward for Dr. Chu—his office, the dayroom, and the dining room. Usually Dr. Chu was everywhere at once. Now he was nowhere. Bones felt his nerves being stretched. Not because he was worried about getting busted himself;

more because he felt compelled to deliver Alice's message as promised.

Bones did the only thing he could think of. He wrote a note and slid it under Dr. Chu's door. He went back to his room, wrapped his red M&M's in toilet paper, and put them in a sock.

It was time to set up for dinner. He shoved the sock in the back of a drawer and rushed to the dining room. *We'll be a couple tonight. Everyone on the ward will know because we'll be holding hands during dinner, gazing into each other's eyes.*

His brain went crazy with the things he'd be able to say to her in front of Teresa, Elsie, Mary-Jane, and the others. The TV had been left on again. An old episode of *Hell's Kitchen* flickered in a mangle of overwrought emotions. *Now those guys need therapy.* He hurriedly set up the tables.

A commercial propagated the dangers of leaving dogs unattended in hot cars—the Valley would cool off later in the week, the forecaster said, down to 101 degrees, though the coast could continue to expect a heavy marine layer.

Bones looked up when Teresa came in. Her eyes were as swollen as the first day he saw her. It looked like she'd been grinding them with salt after an eyewash of pickled beet juice.

She stared at him accusingly, as if she'd caught him pilfering Lucky Charms from the kitchen. "Where've you guys been?" she asked.

Bones shrugged, knowing what she was talking about; he just didn't know how to answer. He stammered, trying to think of something that would be believable. He wasn't coming up with anything.

"Uh, handling an urgent situation," he finally said.

Teresa stood in the middle of the room, slumped. Air wouldn't hold her up much longer. She looked like someone had cut out her heart and pummeled it with a frying pan. And that's pretty much what had happened. "Did I do something wrong...I mean, is Lard mad at me?"

How could he tell her the truth? Without making her feel worse? That Alice had planned an outing that turned into the best day of his life?

"It was sort of last minute," he said, sounding like the dirty rotten liar he was. "But Lard isn't mad at you—I'm sure of that."

Teresa took a few steps backward, bumping a wooden chair, sitting down so hard he expected splinters. "Sometimes I feel like that blue hippo on the cartoon channel. You know the one I mean?"

"Come on, Teresa."

"If I tried to walk on water I'd sink," she said. "I have stubby hippo legs and beady hippo eyes."

"No, you don't."

"I know people stare at me." Her face sank into her hands, making it hard to hear her. "Sometimes I pretend I'm already the perfect weight so I can stop being overwhelmed by what I should and shouldn't eat."

"I've spent most of my life comparing myself to others," Bones said sitting down beside her. "But what's the point? Someone will always be more confident. Smarter, wittier."

"Tanner."

"Exactly."

"I can still fit into the earrings I wore in kindergarten," she said, smiling.

Bones knew what he had to say—it was long overdue. "I'm sorry for not being friendly when I first got here. I was such a jerk."

Then he shrugged.

Teresa shrugged too.

And they both sort of laughed.

This was the longest conversation they'd had one-on-one.

"You wouldn't believe what I used to think about you," she said.

That didn't surprise him. He'd heard it all. Some nights he and Lard talked about the girls like regular guys. Another way to fry time.

"You sure Lard isn't mad at me?" she asked again.

Bones shook his head. "He likes you a lot."

They were quiet awhile.

Teresa picked at her nail polish and watched it flake. Then Nancy appeared with tablecloths, ugly plaid with frayed edges. Bones watched her, thinking she moved too efficiently and without her usual chitchat. He knew something was up—it came from years of experience with shrinks.

When Alice didn't show up for dinner Bones figured she'd gotten busted. He kicked himself for leaving the note, because if she hadn't gotten caught sneaking back into the ward, she sure as hell would have been after Dr. Chu read it. He could only imagine what type of punishment he'd dish up.

"What's the matter?" Teresa asked him.

Bones shrugged, worrying about Alice. It wasn't the first time he'd had to force himself to go through the motions of pretending nothing was wrong.

. . . . . . . . . .

The first thing Bones noticed after crawling into bed after being away from the hospital was the hypoallergenic wintergreen air freshener that had probably never been used in experiments on rats, otherwise it wouldn't have been allowed in institutions that housed human beings.

He lay there in his boxers feeling like he knew where he was in relationship to Alice even when they weren't together. He felt warm in all the places she'd touched him. And even though they didn't go all the way, what they did together, what she did to him, had all the elements to it. Excitement and a secret connection with Alice.

"Teresa's pissed," Lard said from his bed. "I don't blame her."

"Nah, she's more hurt than mad."

"I like her, man," Lard said quietly. "Sure she's a little emotional sometimes, and she has a substantial butt, but hey, we all have our quirks. I really think she's the one. And she feels the same way about me, at least she did until today. That's a first, man, usually it's one-sided. I fucked up. *Bad*."

Bones felt crappy all over again.

"I'm not gonna be one of those jerks who falls asleep after the act," Lard said. "While my girlfriend strokes my forehead worrying that the condom leaked and she's gonna have to raise an army of little Lards."

"You think we'll ever be smart about women?" Bones asked.

"I think we'll always be like this—even when we're thirty."

"Sad, huh?"

"Alice must've gotten nabbed," Lard said.

Bones breathed into the stale air. "I feel guilty that she got caught and we didn't."

"Not me."

Suddenly Bones was back in the elevator with Alice. This time they were both naked. She was licking her lips hungrily while he fed her peanut M&M's from the bag. He let her feed him one—remembering how good they tasted, realizing he must be some kind of freak, because he was getting *hard* all over again.

Bones and Lard were jolted awake sometime before dawn by overhead lights and a maniac in a two-piece jogging suit with turquoise piping. "Get up," Dr. Chu told them.

Bones sat up too fast, nearly falling out of bed. The room was too fluorescent. The voice too loud and authorial.

"Where is she?" Dr. Chu asked.

Bones squinted at him, his heart thudding.

Lard rubbed his eyes. "Who?"

"Don't feed me that crap, Mr. Kowlesky. I know the three of you took off yesterday—and we'll deal with that later, believe me—but Alice never came back and you can't tell me you don't know where she went."

Lard's hair looked like greased crow feathers. "Huh?"

Dr. Chu stood between their beds, his stare heating up the room. He was about to fry them up for breakfast. Pigs in a blanket. "Let me restate this," he said. "Alice came back to the ward but only to clean out her room."

Bones wondered if he was dreaming. Usually when he asked himself that question he woke up.

"As of five minutes ago—exactly five forty-eight a.m.— she hadn't shown up at home either. That means she's been missing for fourteen hours. Her parents have called the police. I expect them here anytime."

Dr. Chu's words were little blowtorches. Bones swallowed hard, choking on ash. He couldn't wrap his brain around it. This couldn't be happening, wasn't supposed to happen. Just last night they were in the elevator. *Alone.* They'd kissed, really kissed—tongues and hot breath. They'd touched. She'd touched him *there.*

"She ran away?" Bones finally said.

When Dr. Chu glared, his eyes were steel barrels of a .44. "Get dressed. In my office. *Now*."

Then he left.

Lard scrambled for his glasses. "Surprise party, my fat ass," he said, fully awake. "It was a going-away party. *Hers.*"

"No, something must have happened—" Bones's heart had shriveled to a dark spot, sloughed off, ready for a biopsy. "Something we don't know about. After the two of us split up in the elevator, something—"

Lard turned to him, his glasses half cocked in an awkward pause. "She planned it, man. Every damned detail."

"No, she—"

"Jesus, how could we be so stupid? Alice doesn't need Tampax. She probably hasn't had a period in years."

Bones stood there so confused about everything.

"That happens to girls who don't have any fat," Lard said, grabbing a pair of pants off the floor. "Time's up. Chu Man's waiting."

Bones put on sweats and slammed out behind him. At the last second, he changed directions and ducked into Alice's room. Bones felt alone and afraid in the lifeless space. Her bed had been stripped to a stained plastic mattress pad. The linens were piled in a heap on the floor. How could the staff be sure she wasn't coming back?

Then he thought, *Maybe Alice stripped it herself.*

He picked up one of the sheets. It smelled like Marlboros and Preparation H.

*Alice.*

*Why?*

*Where?*

He couldn't make sense of it.

Then something caught his eye, in the corner below the window. Her wastebasket, filled with crumpled paper. Bones dropped the sheets onto the bed. He emptied the basket, picked up one piece of paper, smoothed it out, and then another.

*Damn.*

Pages from the magazine she'd painted.

Alice had licked off every bit of Ex-Lax.

Bones couldn't believe it.

Could. Not. Believe. It.

*I should have taken the magazine away from her.*

He sat on the cold floor, staring up at her bulletin board. It was bare too. He went back to the mess on the floor until he found what he was looking for and then checked his watch for today's date. Auditions. Today at the opera house downtown.

Bones hurried back to his room to get Lard's car keys.

To hell with Dr. Chu.

# 28

The day was gray as a low fog marched its fingers over the parking lot, the same type of eerie gloom that crept through vampire novels. Bones shook all over as he climbed into Lard's seat, which was too laid back, more like taking a nap than controlling hundreds of horsepower. He adjusted the mirror and tugged on the seatbelt. It could have looped around his middle and the steering wheel with room left over for Alice.

Bones fumbled the key into the ignition. He backed out looking over his shoulder, shifted into drive, and watched the hospital shrink behind him. His eyes locked on the road, making all the lights on Jefferson, easing from one lane to the other, from one indistinguishable neighborhood to the next. Billboard after billboard. Huge faces peered down with fake smiles.

Alice should have been beside him, smoking and changing radio stations erratically. Instead *How to Shit in the*

*Woods* rode shotgun. The odometer ticked off 226,226 like some kind of ominous sign.

At six forty-five, even on a Saturday morning, the streets were awash with commuters. Coffee-drinkers and women putting on makeup. He counted three Kindles propped on dashboards and five guys shaving with electric razors. The Doodle cornered better than his mom's SUV. It actually dug into the asphalt instead of riding on top of it.

Bones hooked a right at a busy intersection as a big truck whipped by. *Relax*, he told himself. Try to look like any other guy going to work.

The speed limit on surface streets was forty miles-an-hour. Bones figured he could go fifty without getting stopped, unless a cop was below his monthly ticket quota. He turned at the corner of Figueroa where Felix the Cat towered above a Chevrolet dealership.

Bones drove on knowing he wasn't alone in being crazed over Alice's disappearance, also knowing Lard was going to kill him when he found out he stole his car. Grand Theft Auto. That's what the cops would tell his parents.

He kept checking the rearview mirror, as if Chu's posse was on his tail. Two blocks later, he pulled into a driveway next to the opera house. It was seven thirty. Breakfast time at the hospital. His stomach growled.

Just a few weeks ago if his body had started eating itself, it would have been some kind of high. He wouldn't have been able to feel anything else. No pain.

Just the bliss of emptiness. Euphoric. It didn't feel that way this morning.

The fog had some kind of energy to it, like the sun was trying to burn through it. Slowly, the Doodle warmed up. Bones grabbed a bag of Cheese Doodles from Lard's stash in the trunk and counted out five pieces. Forty-five calories. Time moved slower than usual. The snack lasted an hour.

Bones stared out the window. The parking lot was wide, like there was no end to it. He tried to settle back in the seat, but he couldn't settle. Not really. The situation was too unsettling. The rush of escaping the hospital twice in two days and the anticipation of seeing Alice began to give way to fears that this was all some cruel dream brought on by drugs slipped into his orange juice.

He watched an elderly couple amble down the sidewalk holding hands. Their clothes matched down to their thick-soled sneakers and golf visors. He'd bet they walked the same route every day, except Sunday, when the Mr. took the Mrs. to IHOP for blueberry waffles.

Cars slowly began filling the parking lot. Dancers— men and women thin as black ice—got out of beaters as old as the Celica. They were quiet and determined in sweats, scarves, knitted caps. All black, like a congress of undertakers. Dance bags drooped from shoulders. Most carried small ice chests. It was obvious they were fiercely serious about the auditions.

Bones searched faces, trying not to panic. Another half

hour passed without seeing Alice. He thought about her leaping in the halls at night, dancing in her room during the day, working at it all the time. The only ambition Bones ever had was to blend in. To be invisible. Neutral. Non-reasons for goals. A real goal meant moving toward something, like Alice and her dancing.

Maybe she'd gotten here earlier? Or entered through a different door? Yeah, she was probably backstage right now cutting strips of adhesive tape for her toes. Wrapping satin ribbons around her silky ankles. Warming up with *pliés* and *port de bras.*

Bones took another Cheese Doodle from the bag, thinking how different this was from his field trip in the fifth grade when the lot was filled with school buses. He reached around for the M&M's he'd left on the backseat, bummed that he'd already removed the red ones. Instead he climbed stiffly out of the car into the coolness of the morning and began snaking his way through the parking lot.

The wooden doors were heavier than they looked and rooted like trees. He took longer than necessary with his hand on the knob, suddenly apprehensive that Alice would be mad that he'd followed her.

A gush of cold air hit him in the foyer when he passed a refreshment bar with gilded mirrors. Velvet curtains opened into the theater itself. He stood in one place, blinking until his eyes adjusted, then made his way down the side aisle unnoticed. In the front row, men and women sat in dark suits holding clipboards. With everyone talking at once, Bones wondered how they knew who was saying what.

Piano music trickled in from some unseen place. An old man with a Van Dyke goatee wielded a cane on center stage. The man hollered, "Cue music!"

Bones watched as two dancers appeared like magic from the wings.

The girl moved silent as a shadow, then, suddenly, she seemed to levitate, her pointe shoes barely touching the stage. In one effortless movement, the guy lifted her above his head and they spun in a dizzy circle.

Alice had tried explaining this to him, this exact movement, but seeing it was the only way to fully understand the combination of strength and grace.

The old man pounded the floor with his cane. "No! It is still wrong! No matter how many times you do it! Why do you insist on acknowledging the audience?"

The dancers seemed to shrink in front of him, attentively sweating.

"And your *port de bras*! No one will care anything about your steps if your arms do not float through whipped cream!"

The pair nodded meekly. "Can we try again?" the guy asked.

The old man dismissed them with a wave of his cane. "There is no time for dancers who refuse to learn. Next!"

Bones felt bad for them but kept walking down the worn carpet, making his way toward a door that he remembered led backstage. He opened the door, relieved that no one was paying attention to him, and stepped into a confusion of limbs and spandex.

The guys were either bare-chested or wore sleeveless T-shirts. Their muscles were ripped. He spotted the girl who'd just left the stage, sitting on the floor untying her shoes and crying quietly. Then she began moving her arms through something invisible, probably whipped cream.

Bones stepped around an older woman doing the splits against a wall, then by a guy icing his knee with a bag of frozen peas. One dancer was talking on a cell phone and laughing. Another was contemplating the remains of a banana. Febreze was sprayed into shoes.

Bones smelled the smells—Bengay and Preparation H—and listened to the hum of brittle chatter. And then he saw her—standing in the corner away from the others—delicate as a ladyfinger.

*Alice.*

Her back was to him, one hand on her ankle, her leg a perfect arc over her head. Little pearls of sweat glistened on her shoulders and neck.

"Alice," he whispered, making his way toward her.

Dr. Chu, Lard, and her parents—everyone had been wrong. This wasn't about the pill of fame taking away her pain. Alice was a dancer, an artist pursuing her dreams. Pure and simple. Why couldn't they understand that?

Bones reached out, gently touching her shoulder. She

swung around, obviously startled. Her lips moved, nothing else. "Excuse me?" she said.

Her voice didn't sound right; it was too deep. Where were her almond eyes? Her sexy smile? The aroma of sugarless gum? He shook his head to make her cinnamon freckles materialize.

"You're not Alice," he muttered as his throat closed up. Tight. Little ice picks stabbed at it. His feet tried to move. Stuck. There was nothing left in him. Nothing.

· · · · · · · · · ·

Bones wasn't aware of driving back to the hospital. He could barely hold the steering wheel—dying inside an orange Celica with expired plates. He'd started to believe thoughts were real things, but if they were only real in his head, then they weren't real at all.

The only empty parking spot had a pole with a sign attached to it showing a wheelchair. Perfect for a three-thousand pound Cheese Doodle with a moribund driver.

His tears came slowly.

# 29

Once inside the hospital, Bones moved swiftly down the corridor, intent on snatching the sheets from Alice's bed for himself. He'd remake his bed and sleep tangled in her essence until she came back. *She always does*, he told himself.

But for some strange reason, he wasn't surprised her bed had been remade. Crisp sheets tucked in too tight. The sheets he'd planned on taking to his room—her sheets, the sheets he'd left in a pile on the floor a few hours ago—had vanished. Not even Nureyev looked down from the wall to say Alice had lived and breathed in this space.

Bones checked Alice's closet and dresser frantically, unsure what he was looking for. Then he hit her bathroom, kneeling on the cold tile in the shower. Pine Sol stung his nose. His eyes burned. Not a single strand of strawberry blond hair.

He squeezed his eyes shut and folded up on himself,

held down by the everyday hospital racket resonating from outside. He figured he'd been crumpled up long enough when he'd lost all feeling in his legs. If only he could numb his heart. It seemed he was always saying good-bye to pieces of Alice.

Bones forced himself to get up and caught a glimpse of himself in her mirror. His image looked deflated, his oxygen out on loan. He'd always had food or the lack of it to focus on in times like this. But he didn't want to eat. He didn't want *not* to eat. Only one person could give him any kind of comfort, and for the millionth time today he felt the lack of her presence.

*Missing her hurt as much as loving her. But I will never stop loving her, not as long as I live. And I will never stop dreaming about her, never stop waiting for her, never stop looking for her. Never.*

But the truth stretched out in front of him: loving her hadn't been enough.

Not enough for her.

Lard was right; Alice had thrown herself a going-away party. She'd given him a parting gift in the elevator. Bones had to admit it. No he didn't. Couldn't. Wouldn't.

Bones barely made it though lunch, gagging down the extra four ounces of Ensure Nancy gave him to make up for missing breakfast. He sat alone with his back to the room and tuned out the meaningless chatter. The weirdest thing of all was Dr. Chu hadn't called him to his office for the umpteen infractions over the last two days.

Bones stayed in his room as much as possible. He lay on his bed, floating in the sweet memory of the elevator, halfway between heaven and hell. A void where it didn't matter that nothing mattered.

Even Lard moved through space noiselessly.

They didn't know what to say or do.

Neither of them slept that night.

It was as if they'd had their own private meeting where they'd mutually decided to check out for a few days—like their brains were on overload and were shutting down to recharge. Sometimes when there's so much to think about it's better to be quiet.

Just when the dream-state seemed to be lifting, Bones was summoned by Dr. Chu. Bones stood lifeless in the cramped office space facing a pair of navy blue uniforms who introduced themselves as Officers Brunner and Manor. Badges pinned beneath dull expressions.

"We need to ask you a few questions," Officer Brunner said. He was short with bushy gray hair. A roll of fat hung over his belt. "Would you like your parents here?"

Bones shook his head. "I just want to help."

"Answer their questions as honestly as you can, Jack," Dr. Chu said, failing miserably at a supportive smile. "Okay?"

"I want to find her more than anyone else," Bones said.

"I'm sure your roommate"—Officer Brunner frowned at his notes as if unable to read his own handwriting—"Mr. Bowelesky told you about our chat the other day."

"Mr. Kowlesky." Bones corrected him. "He mentioned it." Lard said he'd been grilled by two of LA's finest. *Like I was part of a subversive terrorist plot or something*, he'd said.

"Accordingly…" Manor flipped pages in his notebook, fountain pen poised as if ready to inflict pain. "You and Mr. Kowlesky spent the afternoon with Miss Graham before she left."

Brunner took a wide, flat-footed stance. "If she did indeed leave under her own volition," he said.

Bones let it sink in. "You don't think she left on her own?"

"We have to consider all the possibilities," Brunner said.

"We understand Miss Graham is extremely sick and only recently released from Intensive Care," Manor said, tapping his pen on his pad. His shaved head and small gold earring glinted under the fluorescent light. "Were you aware of her heart problems?"

Bones felt all eyes on him. "But she was getting better," he stammered. "Almost back to normal…"

"It's difficult to imagine—" Brunner began.

Manor stepped closer, picking it up from there. "No, more like impossible—"

"—to understand how someone so sick could plan her own exit as well as execute it," Brunner concluded.

Bones couldn't focus under the weight of what he was hearing. He stared down at the carpet, stuck on *heart problems.* "She had that ventricular thing," he said. "She told me lots of people have it—that it wasn't a big deal."

Bones looked at Dr. Chu who'd been in the background fingering his soul patch. "Ventricular tachycardia is potentially life-threatening," he said, moving into the fray. "It can lead to sudden death."

"But she said—"

Brunner pinned him accusingly. "Why would you and your roommate take Miss Graham on a joyride?"

"What about that, Jack?" Dr. Chu said.

"She seemed fine. Normal. In a great mood. There wasn't really a plan. We just felt like getting out for a while— all we did was drive around and listen to music."

"Where did you go yesterday morning?" Brunner asked. "After you learned Miss Graham was missing?"

Bones took a breath.

Manor nodded, that universal signal to go on.

"I thought I knew where she was," Bones said. "I remembered the dance auditions at the opera house downtown. I thought she might have gone there."

Bones could tell Manor wasn't buying it, wasn't even pretending to buy it. He expected Dr. Chu to rip him a new one for not telling him about the audition sooner.

"Then someone must have seen you." Brunner again.

"Yes. I mean no. Well, maybe."

"Which is it?" Manor stared at him.

Bones wasn't sure what to expect first, handcuffs or the Miranda rights. "I didn't really talk to anyone," he said.

The officers looked bored, ready to move on. "We'll be back," Manor said and turned on a polished heel.

Bones hesitated. "There might be something else."

Brunner faced him, a cat over a gopher hole.

Bones knew he had to tell them about the magazine pages. "I found them in her wastebasket." He hoped the information would encourage them to amp up the search. "She licked off the Ex-Lax."

"Why would she do something like that?" Manor asked.

"It's an old trick," Bones said quietly.

The two men studied him quizzically, seemingly convinced he was telling the truth. Who would make up something like that?

# 30

As if things weren't crappy enough, Dr. Chu called Bones's parents and told them about the two unauthorized trips from the hospital, both within a twenty-four hour period. A family meeting was scheduled for the following afternoon.

It was good to see his mom and dad—but a little strange in a space too small for so much worry (him) and disappointment (them). He liked his mom's new short hair and jean jacket. His dad sipped hot tea from a Styrofoam cup.

Bones was still shook up from being questioned by the cops. He shifted from foot to foot, not easy since he was sitting down. He gripped the arms of the chair and told his parents that someone he cared about was missing.

The words tumbled out in a stream so sudden, even the framed posters were listening. "I thought I knew where she was." His voice shook but somehow he managed to get it all out. "So I took Lard's car."

"That girl?" his mom asked. "The one we saw family night?"

Bones nodded. "Alice."

Dr. Chu had dark circles under his eyes and he blinked too fast, as if afraid of breaking down. Bones had never seen him like this. He studied Bones from the other side of his desk, arms crossed as if he'd caught him in another lie. And that's exactly how Bones felt, like everything he'd had with Alice was a lie.

"It looks like she ran away," Bones mumbled. "But the police aren't so sure."

Another miserably long second passed while his mom fiddled with a button on her jacket. Then she cleared her throat. Bones knew she was working up to something.

"I starved myself for a week," she finally said. "I wanted to know what it felt like."

His dad scratched the stubble on his chin. "You did what?"

"It was an experiment." His mom looked at him. "You were working late and we weren't having meals together. I'd have a cup of coffee and a half grapefruit for breakfast, maybe a green salad for dinner. I was completely exhausted and had a constant headache. I'd wake up in the middle of the night starving."

Bones didn't know how he could feel any worse but he did.

"Then something started to happen—I'd hear voices in my head. *Come on,* they said. *Come on, you can do it.* The longer I stayed away from the kitchen the more powerful I felt, like it was some sort of victory."

There was a long silence.

"It's hard to watch our kids make mistakes and not want to fix them," Dr. Chu said.

His mom sighed, question in her eyes. "But not if trying to fix things keeps them sick. I hope that doesn't sound too harsh."

At that moment Bones thought his mom was the smartest person in the world. He could have done more thinking about his own problems while he'd been in here, but he'd done enough to know that he didn't want to come back once he got out.

He wanted to get well.

He knew that's what it came down to.

He wanted to be his mom and dad's son again.

He wanted to be his sister's brother.

And he wanted to be a whole person when they found Alice.

Bones watched his dad cross his legs, careful not to kick the desk. He knew what he was thinking before he said it. "What about our son?"

There could be all kinds of answers to this question.

They'd all begin with *Jack left hospital grounds on two consecutive days without permission, an obvious and blatant violation...he'll now be confined to his room with an ankle monitor. House arrest.*

Bones kept waiting for Dr. Chu to remind him that he'd

once been a teenager and therefore understood what Bones was going through. *It's just a phase*, he'd say. *Don't worry, you'll outgrow it.*

Dr. Chu sighed a little uncertainly. "More than half of our patients fully recover. They go to college, get married, raise families. Have meaningful careers," he said. "Jack has reached a point where he should start thinking about what he's going to do when he leaves here."

His dad set both feet on the ground. "Private therapy?"

"That's one option," Dr. Chu said. He reached for a folder, pausing to thumb through it. "The hospital holds group therapy once a week in the basement for former patients. It's a great group of kids. What do you say, Jack?"

Bones thought of all the things he'd done since he'd been in the program. Things he never thought he'd be able to do. Then he nodded, because he didn't know what else to do, and because he wanted to stay connected to the people he'd met here, and just when he thought Dr. Chu might seem more human without PhD attached to his name, Dr. Chu slipped a contract from the folder and asked Bones to sign it.

Essentially Bones agreed not to leave the ward under any circumstances unless accompanied by a staff member.

And that included the roof.

No problem.

Who wanted to go up there now?

. . . . . . . . . .

Other than meals and regularly scheduled activities Bones

stayed in his room reading, working on exercises, writing to his family. Now he sat in the dayroom with his back to the window moving tiles around the Scrabble board. S-V-E-L-T-E. He rearranged them. L-O-V-E and D-E-S-I-R-E.

Next turn.

He spelled H-O-P-E-L-E-S-S and removed the last four letters.

For the last four years, Bones had lived for the gnawing feeling of hunger in his stomach—because it meant his body was consuming itself. Now the empty feeling terrified him—because it was associated with loss and longing. He was more afraid than ever that he'd never see Alice again.

Another two days passed like a slow moving cloud.

Nighttime was worse.

Bones listened to the sound of movement in the hall outside his room. Water sloshed in a bucket. A mop smacked the baseboard. He imagined Unibrow sipping Ensure from a bottle concealed in a brown paper bag, stolen from the locked cupboard where cases of supplements were stored.

As much as Bones was irritated by the existence of Unibrow, he thought the mass the guy displaced was somehow less threatening than that of someone who actually cared, like Nancy for instance, who left Bones feeling like he'd disappointed her.

Bones rolled over and grabbed his pillow. Rolled over again, punched it. Fear consumed him. Sometimes it had a sound of its own, like one of those whistles only dogs can hear.

He had the sense Lard was awake. "What time is it?"

"Tomorrow," he said.

Lard shifted and his bedsprings groaned. "Alice is—" he started and stopped.

Bones waited.

"She conned everyone. Her parents, her doctors. She even conned us, man."

Bones wanted to slug him.

"It's the truth, man. Maybe the only truth."

Somewhere deep inside Bones knew he was right.

He and Lard had spent endless hours trying to figure things out. Why she left; where she went.

"She isn't anorexic because she's a ballerina," Lard said. "Anymore than she's a ballerina because she's anorexic."

"Post hoc, ergo propter hoc," Bones said.

"You keep talking like that and I'm gonna wash your mouth out with soap."

"It means, A occurred, then B. Therefore A caused B," Bones said. "Let's just say that more teens are going to church than ever before. Yet unwanted teen pregnancy is on the rise. That would mean churches are corrupting today's youth, hypothetically speaking."

Lard gave the kind of snort he was famous for.

"Philosophy one-oh-one," Bones said.

Then they spent too much time talking about Elsie, who they agreed would always be a cow, and Mary-Jane, who'd have a better chance in life if she'd stop hanging around

Elsie. It was stupid gossip. But what were they supposed to do when they were locked up like monkeys in a zoo?

Besides, they had to *talk* about something to keep from *thinking*. Sometimes it worked, for about thirty seconds. Then Lard fired up his chainsaw. The nasal strips Alice had given him were useless. Lard sawed. Bones stacked, question upon question.

*Why hasn't she tried to get ahold of us?*

Bones wondered when the idea of running away had first come to her. She'd planned everything so carefully. But she had to feel bad about the way she did it. She had the same memories he had.

*Maybe she can't contact us?*

Finally it was just too much. Bones couldn't think about it anymore—thinking and feeling was too much to deal with. Thinking itself was paralyzing. He clung to his sheet begging for sleep and closed his eyes thinking about CRAP.

Back when he'd read the first pages, he thought George was writing a love story, a tribute to Alice and his feelings for her. That he'd wanted to create a special world for her, a world safe from neurotic parents and inflexible therapists, where she'd be free to pursue her art anyway she chose.

Now he knew George's feelings for Alice were only part of it. George wrote his story as much out of frustration as anything—he wanted Alice to get better as much as everyone else. And like everyone else, he didn't know how to help her.

Bones got up and went to his desk for the pages of

CRAP he'd gathered so far. Writing by flashlight, he took over where George had left off, feeling an urgency to add more to the story for Alice, and realized George hadn't been hiding it from Dr. Chu. He'd been stashing it for Alice, betting she'd come back to the hospital like she always did and find it while hiding something of her own.

Bones and Alice passed enormous billboards, *Long Live His Excellency! Fear the Enemy! Stateland or Death!* His Excellence was never understanding, never merciful. He moved swiftly to punish those who disobeyed him.

"Illustrious," Bones said, his lips pressing hers for the first time.

They set up a primitive camp in the bowels of a demolished theme park, where a decapitated Alice in Wonderland lolled in a cracked teacup. They made nightly trips foraging for anything useful—hauling off broken bits of this and that, even a squashed case of Twinkies, which tasted pretty good considering the expiration date of decades past.

Bones knew he had to figure out how they were going to sustain themselves. Sadly, the golden sponge cakes with their creamy filling were long gone; their sticky wrappers licked clean.

Alice squeezed her eyes shut. "Hope is just a dream waiting to happen," she said.

Bones wanted his future self to say something equally brilliant. But everything he wrote lacked originality. He tore up page after page, frustrated, then settled on:

Bones and Alice were in dire need of a tube feeding, although they found exploring each other's curves and hollows more interesting than discussing wasting flesh.

Late one night Alice wept over something she couldn't explain. Bones thought her tears were opalescent from the absorption of his fluids. It must have nutrients, he thought, because her breasts were overflowing with the same milky substance.

Bones and Alice hid during the daylight hours when only those with Oxygen Permits were allowed above ground. Time passed, days turning into weeks that fell one on top of another.

He played his guitar, expressing ideas about a community of artists, arranging his words in an elaborate language. "Your music showers me with images," Alice said, working pigment into wet plaster. "Keep singing and I'll paint it."

He sang about his passion for his soul mate, Alice, while she languished over her latest fresco, *A Ballet for Bones*.

Another endlessly long day.
Bones was tired. So tired.

# 31

Bones knew he'd gained another five flippin' pounds without the flippin' scale telling him he was a flippin' one-hundred-fifteen flippin' pounds—because the waistband of his sweats was leaving an indelible ring on his flabby skin and choking off his belly button.

He stood on the overturned trashcan peering into the treacherous mirror with its unexpected dangers. Sometimes the glass sucked you in, and you were swimming alone in glass and more than a little bit afraid. Sometimes life itself sucked you in like that. Today his reflection told him what he already knew. If he didn't buy bigger pants, he'd be chewed in half by insatiable elastic.

Bones turned on the hot water in the sink until steam obliterated his augmenting self. He knew he didn't have a choice, standing in front of his closet a minute later studying the jeans his mom had brought for him. Relaxed, yet classic. Slightly faded. Ragged cuffs.

Bones shed his trusty sweats and stepped into one leg, then the other, yanking on the waist, worried it wouldn't make it over his hips. He refused to look at the size as the jeans fought back. Unfortunately Bones won. At least the jean material was soft; his mom must've washed them in fabric softener.

Lard set Rachael Ray aside. "Not too bad, more like you've got an ass. Girls like an ass, man. It gives them something to hang onto."

"Yeah?"

"Trust me."

"Never."

Later in the dayroom, Elsie said, "Hey there. You look good with a little meat on your bone."

Bones couldn't believe she was checking out his package.

· · · · · · · · · ·

Overall, the Eating Disorders Unit was in a shitty mood. Except for Elsie, who didn't count, no one had slept all that much since Alice disappeared. Dr. Chu had somehow managed to be both distracted and verbose during therapy sessions. He'd never carried his cell phone with him before. Now he answered anxiously on the first ring.

Only Unibrow seemed immune to the low spirits on the fourth floor, indifferent as a head of lettuce.

As the days wore on, Bones felt like he was becoming lost in the memory of Alice's eyes, her touch, her scent.

Sometimes he got up in the middle of the night, hit the stairs, and wandered aimlessly around different floors, invariably ending up on the sixth floor, where Alice asked him to tell her a story. He wondered if she had the bear with her. Other times he'd run into nurses taking care of nighttime business. They were either too tired or busy to question him.

· · · · · · · · · ·

It was one of those days when Bones only thought about Alice and why she'd left and where she might have gone and what she might be doing every other second. He and Lard had talked about it ad nauseam and they came to the conclusion that she had to be okay, wherever she was. Otherwise— they'd worked frantically to convince each other—one of them would have heard something to the contrary.

Then on Friday night, while Bones was finishing a letter to his sister, Lard appeared in the doorway. "Do you know the difference between an alcoholic and someone with food issues?"

"How many guesses do I get?" Bones asked.

"A drunk can give up his drug, like cold turkey."

"I suppose."

"It might be about as easy as unscrambling an egg—but at least he won't die."

Bones didn't get where this was going. "Sorry, you lost me."

"What's a person with an eating disorder supposed to give up?" Lard asked.

"I give up."

*"Food."*

"I get the analogy," Bones said. "Sort of."

"Guess it wouldn't be much of a problem for anorexics."

"More like nirvana."

Lard grabbed his lunchbox. "Maybe I'm the one who's been a contemptuous jerk."

It wasn't like Lard wanted a response; it was more like he was saying it out loud because he needed to hear what it sounded like.

Lard waved his lunchbox. "Wanna know what's in here?"

Bones smiled at the ridiculous sight. "Only if you want to tell me."

Lard flipped the latch, letting the lid fall open. Packages of Twinkies tumbled out. "I've been carrying around Twinkies the whole time I've been lecturing you," he said. "I'm like a recovering alcoholic who keeps a bottle of Jack Daniels on the kitchen counter as a sick way of testing my willpower."

Bones stared at the Twinkies. "Maybe it's more like a reminder of who you used to be," he said. "So you won't go back to being that person."

Lard flattened a Twinkie with the sole of his boot.

*Smash!*

"That's why I didn't take the magazine away from Alice."

*Smash!*

"Because I had goddamned Twinkies in my lunchbox."

*Smash!*

"Get rid of them for me, okay?"

Bones winced at the oozing cream filling. "I've been wondering about something else."

"Lay it on me, man. I'm already in a shitty mood."

"How did you get my medical files when I first got here?" Bones asked. "What'd you do, hack into Chu's computer?"

Lard stood in doorway, effectively sealing his voice inside the room. "I found a set of keys in the kitchen. It was just a hunch, and sure enough, one of them was to his office."

"No way."

"Wanna guess his password?"

*"God?"*

"Yeah."

"You're kidding me."

"Yeah."

"I've been thinking, if we could read Alice's files…" Bones was still working it out in his mind. "Maybe we'd find something about her we don't know, something to tell us where she might have gone. Her address…maybe if we could talk to her parents—"

"You think they'd talk to us?" Lard ran a hand through his unruly hair. "Knowing it was my car we used that day?"

Bones knew he was right.

"Besides Chu Man changed the lock right after I found his keys," Lard said. "He would've changed his pass-word too."

"Probably."

Bones was left with a dozen squashed sponge cakes, wondering if he should flush them down the toilet. First he'd have to unwrap them. He was sitting on the floor, scissors suspended like a dagger when Nancy came in.

"I have your new menus," she said, stopping mid-stride.

Bones glanced up, their eyes locking.

"If I don't see what you're doing I won't have to report it," she said.

No one would believe he'd sneaked Twinkies onto the EDU. And that's what he told Nancy.

"You don't have to explain," she said.

Nancy stood there silently, swaying awkwardly from one sensible shoe to the other. Bones watched her, thinking about her lack of presence in the days since Alice disappeared. *She's been avoiding me.*

That's when he finally knew. He read it in the dullness of her eyes and felt scared all over again. His voice pierced the silence, "Nancy, you know where Alice is, don't you?"

Nancy sighed then swished by the beds and desks to the open window. "Yes, but…" She was staring out across the parking lot and talking away from him so he had to strain to hear. "I'm sorry, Bones. It isn't just doctor-patient confidentiality…Alice is a minor and she was under our care when she left."

She turned to him, closed her eyes a moment, and opened them again. "You saw her parents…what they're like."

The look on her face gave him a sinking feeling. He remembered that night on the roof with Alice when she talked about the bus stop in front of the hospital. *Wouldn't it be fun to get on a bus and not know where you'd end up?* She could have gone anywhere.

"Did she take a bus?" he asked.

Nancy sort of nodded. "She bought a bus ticket to New York." She chose her words carefully. "Police found her at a Greyhound bus station in LA. She was passed out in the bathroom…I'm sorry I can't tell you more, Bones. We're just so grateful she's alive."

*Alive?*

What did that mean? He'd thought she might have gone to San Francisco to dance on Fisherman's Wharf for spare change or had been kidnapped by Romanian gypsies. "I never thought she wasn't okay."

Nancy looked at him now, really looked at him. "It's this damned disorder, it's so emotional, and at the same time biological. The two are so entangled. Sometimes people just never resolve—" She sighed, stopping herself. "How're you doing with all this?"

Bones couldn't answer. His grief was like the latest strain of bubonic plague. Zero mercy to it. Whoever said time heals all wounds should be drawn and quartered. His body ached from eleven days of heartbreaking worry.

"Sorry," Nancy said again.

And this time she left.

Bones stabbed a Twinkie with the scissors and flung it out the window. Alice must be in a hospital somewhere. That had to be it. If she were somewhere in this hospital, news would have leaked out.

Bones scooped up the rest of the petroleum byproduct and let it sail out the window. He had to get his hands on a phone. He'd call every hospital in Los Angeles County if he had to. Or he'd take Lard's car. Yeah, that was a better idea. He had to *see* her.

He dug through Lard's desk searching for his keys.

· · · · · · · · · ·

"What'd you think, man?" Lard said as he emptied the dishwasher. "That I'd leave my keys lying around? After you parked in a handicapped spot? You're lucky the Doodle didn't get towed."

"I was desperate," Bones said.

"And another thing, the steering wheel was orange. You should definitely use a napkin when stealing a person's car and eating his snacks."

Bones sat down across from Teresa, vaguely aware of the fish on the table between them. It lay in a tray of ice chips, cold and dead. Teresa was tearing sheets of aluminum foil from a long roll, carefully measuring each square.

"Alice is in a hospital somewhere," Bones said.

Teresa muttered, *"Coma."*

Bones felt his heart slide into the ice chips. Nancy hadn't said anything about a coma.

"How do you know?" Lard asked her.

"I overheard Dr. Chu on the phone when I went to his office to ask about—you know," she said, not looking at them. "I'm pretty sure he was talking to one of her parents."

Lard butt-bumped the dishwasher door closed. "Why didn't you tell us?"

"Because there isn't anything we can do," she said quietly.

Bones hated her for saying what he should have known. He was on his feet, ready to hit the road. "What else did you hear?"

"I don't know." Teresa started to cry. "She's in ICU. No one can see her but family." She sounded frightened, like she did that night on the roof after the family therapy fiasco. "I think it's worse than the other times."

Bones was in front of Lard. "I need your keys!"

Lard stared back. "Chu Man confiscated them."

"You're lying!" Bones shouted at him.

"They're locked in his drawer."

Bones didn't believe him. "Don't you want to know what hospital she's in? That this is all an elaborate joke and she's sitting up in bed watching soap operas and eating bonbons. *Don't you care about her anymore*?"

"What're you gonna do? Break down the doors to ICU?"

"You have a better idea?"

Lard backed away, slowly shaking his head. "There's gotta be two-hundred hospitals in LA county—that would take days. Maybe weeks. You…Me…" His voice had a sharp edge to it. "We can't help her, man. We never could."

Frantically, Bones started rummaging through drawers. Peelers, graters, whisks, bottle-stoppers. He felt Lard's beefy hands on his shoulders before he was spun around. "I'm telling you, man, I don't have the keys."

Bones ripped away from him. "Fuck you, Mr. Already-Has-a-Girlfriend-and-Doesn't-Care-about-His-Friends-Anymore!"

Lard ripped right back. "Or maybe I care just as much about you as I do about her!"

Bones didn't want to hear it.

He hit the stairs at full speed, powering to the top, hyperventilating, as he raced through the storage area, vaulting over carpet remnants and paint cans.

Just before he reached the door to the roof, he tripped over a bucket and collided face-first with the doorknob. Since he didn't die immediately he swore and clutched at his eye. His whole face throbbed. He swore again and pushed through the door, stumbling headlong onto the roof, trying to focus and wondering what life would be like blind.

# 32

Bones squinted at the intensely blue sky through a blur of stars. He felt his face. No blood. But the throbbing in his eye was intense. He put his hand over one eye and blinked, then the other. He'd have a serious shiner, but at lease he wasn't blind.

He picked his way over a jumble of conduits. The zucchini had grown like crazy in their neglect. Everything else drooped, begging for water. Lard hadn't been up here either for the same reason. Memories were like vinegar spurting from an open vein.

While searching for the watering can he noticed the folding chairs, purposefully arranged, like someone had planned it. *Alice.* Her yoga mat was unrolled. Four candles sat on top holding the edges down. She'd even left a book of matches. *Ocean View Suites.*

Bones felt like he was walking backward and forward at the same time, drowning in an empty space that should have been Alice. He struck a match and lit a candle. Vanilla. Then he sat back on his heels, blinking at the unsteady flicker. He pictured Alice asleep and wondered if a person in a coma had dreams. He hoped she had her ballet slippers with her.

He thought about love and fear and how closely they were related. Love takes your breath away. But the fear of losing someone you love is a barbed arrow that pierces your heart, and it hurts so much it takes your breath away too. Bones had to force himself to breathe. He got up slowly, filled the watering can, and gave everything a good soak.

He used to feel the same way Alice did, like the hospital was a prison controlled by a ruthless warden and his minions. But now, here on the roof, the EDU seemed more real than the outside world. More real than high school and grades and who's doing what with whom on a Saturday night. More real than all his insecurities and his incurable loneliness.

He had to say it aloud. "You know I'd be with you if I could…"

Talking like that kept him weirdly calm.

He imagined her snarky voice. "Cut it out!"

Bones blew out the candle and, as lame as it seemed, he made a wish. Then he turned the front of his T-shirt into a sack, filled it with ripe vegetables, and aimed his miserable self down the stairs to tell Lard he didn't mean what he'd said earlier.

. . . . . . . . . .

The next day Bones leaned over the bathroom sink to examine the damage to his face in the mirror. A condor egg filled the space where his eye should have been. It hurt like hell. *Twenty-twenty vision is probably overrated*, he thought.

Bones kept insisting he ran into a door. "I swear."

Dr. Chu didn't buy it.

Nancy brought him an icepack.

Lard liked everyone thinking he'd done the deed.

Bones stumbled through the rest of the day. Literally. Only having one good eye messed with his equilibrium. He couldn't seem to make his legs track in a straight line. He'd sideswiped enough walls to make his shoulders ache.

He wandered to the dayroom to see if anything was happening. It was empty but the TV had been left on. One of those prison dramas where bad-asses swore on their grandmother's grave that they'd never be back once they got out. But after release most of them would return to the same crime-ridden, drug-infested neighborhoods as before— hang out with the same lowlife scum and fall into the same destructive habits. They'd be back in prison within a year.

Bones thought about what he'd learned the last couple of weeks. Sometimes he didn't think it was much. Other times it felt like volumes. He knew this much: someone who did the same thing, the same way, over and over, and expected a different outcome was kidding himself. It might even be a form of insanity. If a person wanted his life to be different, to be *better*, then he had to *do things* differently.

..........

Dr. Chu's office door was open. "Excuse me," Bones said.

Dr. Chu glanced up from a mess of papers on his desk. "How're you doing, Jack?"

"I had a question about the outpatient program."

"Sure, come on in."

Bones collapsed into the chair. "Is it okay if I try it while I'm still a patient? Or do I have to wait until I check out?"

Dr. Chu rearranged his smile. "That's unusual but not a bad idea. As a matter of fact, I just signed off on your bathroom door."

"Bathroom?" Bones asked.

"It's okay for you and David to close your door to conduct your personal business in private. It's not a privilege we extend lightly, believe me, and only after a lengthy discussion with the staff."

That meant they trusted them not to throw up in the shower or whatever.

"The decision was nearly unanimous," Dr. Chu said.

"Can we hook up the fan?" Bones asked.

"These bathrooms don't have fans," he said. "Hospital policy."

Dr. Chu, seeming to have exhausted his compassion for the moment, returned to his papers.

. . . . . . . . . .

The next night after a dinner of unidentifiable meat, half a baked potato with low-fat sour cream, steamed vegetables, and the usual brick-and-mortar roll, Bones followed Dr. Chu and Lard to the elevator to a conference room.

"Nancy will come down after the meeting to take you back," Dr. Chu said and left.

The door to the conference room was ajar. "Follow me," Lard said.

Bones took a deep breath. "Where have I heard that before?"

# 33

Six or seven people milled around a card table crowded with a coffee urn, pitcher of pink lemonade, and a tray of cut-up fruit so uninteresting Bones knew it didn't come from Gumbo's knife. A long conference table exuded power and took up most of the room. The leather chairs around it looked sturdy enough to hold whatever was about to be dumped on them.

One guy looked like someone Bones would cross the street to avoid. His shaved head had some scary tattoos. "I'm Ramon," the guy said, extending his hand. He was ripped, probably an athlete. "But I used to be Rake."

"Lard."

"Bones." He tried to match name tags with body types: Elizabeth (cute and chubby—probably a recovering bulimic), Daphne (ditto), Cynthia (obviously ex-anorexic), Christy (impossible to tell), Phil (definitely a snacks-in-front-of-the-TV-over-eater).

Bones had hoped to see Eve, posing in pearls as the poster girl for recovery. "I never would've been brave enough to come down here while I was in the program," Daphne said, smiling. "Does Dr. Chu still wear those lame ties?"

Bones smiled back. "With gravy stains."

He reminded himself why he was here and tried not to act nervous while he poured lemonade into a Dixie cup and looked for a saltshaker. He noticed a whiteboard with a diagram of the human brain. An area was shaded in and labeled *body awareness*. Oddly enough, it was larger than the parts of the brain that controlled speech, taste, smell, and hearing.

"Hey, Julia." Phil waved to a girl in the hall. "We're about to get started."

The girl frowned and pushed her walker into the room like she was in a bizarre six-legged race. "My dad drives like an old lady," she said.

The walker reminded Bones of the one his mom used after knee surgery. Only this one was a swirl of color. Julia's hair looked like charcoal briquettes, black with red tips. She wore paisley high-tops sans laces, electric blue socks, and plaid board shorts. A mermaid snaked up her calf. Bones liked it.

Julia stopped at the first chair and shrugged out of her backpack. She fiddled with the zipper and took out dangerous looking knitting needles and camouflage-colored yarn.

Ramon told everyone to take a seat, opened a worn-looking pamphlet, and read guidelines about respecting each other's points of view. Then everyone introduced himself or herself: first name; particular disorder, anorexic, bulimic, compulsive overeater; how they were coping with life on the outside by trying to ditch their former world of extremes and navigate the much more difficult road of middle ground.

When the regulars finished, Bones realized the ice cubes in his cup were rattling. He set the cup on the floor and wiped his damp hands on his jeans. This was going to be tougher than he thought. "I'm still trying to make sense of it," he began slowly. "I was only trying to lose a few pounds…"

"It might sound like a cliché but it really does get better." Daphne again. "You'll never have to go back to the dark side."

Bones nodded, somewhat grateful, because even though it was the usual banter, it was what he needed to hear at this particular moment. The next twenty minutes was lost to horror stories about recovery, battles big and small, won and lost. Problems with insensitive families or friends who just didn't get it.

Ramon raised his hand halfway. "I'm having a hard time with dates."

"Dried or fresh?"

"Pitted?"

"Packaged?"

Everyone laughed, which helped take the edge off.

Ramon stared past them until he remembered whatever it was he was about to say. "So I like this girl, and I take her to a nice place downtown, but all she does is pick at her food," he said. "I don't eat much either, 'cause I don't want her to think I'm a pig."

"Restaurants are tricky," Julia said, laying yarn across her lap. "Movies are worse, all that greasy popcorn."

"Artificial flavorings give me the runs." Lard knew when to go for a laugh. "You might as well ask for Pennzoil."

"Quaker State," Phil said managing a straight face.

Julia's hands were busy working her knitting needles. "There are tons of things to do on a date that don't involve food," she said. "A stroll in the park at sunset. Take stale bread for the ducks."

The room waited for more.

"Check the newspaper for openings at art galleries," she said. "Sometimes they have live music."

"Girls like that stuff?" Ramon asked.

"I'm not the only female who cozies up to a little ingenuity." Julia's needles were on fire. She'd added another foot to her long, skinny scarf. Who was it for, a giraffe? "Someone start a phone list for Bones and Lard, and any of you can call me if you get stuck for ideas. Anytime, any weather. I'm freakin' brilliant when it comes to thunderstorms."

Bones listened. This was the sort of meeting he'd hoped for. Where people didn't just make excuses for binging on pizza or obsessing on M&M's. Where people did more than communicate through sighs and sobs, zoning in and out of self-absorbed unhappiness. A group where everyone felt safe enough to be him or herself, talk about their issues, and share ideas that were actually helpful.

"I hated Dr. Chu when I was upstairs," Cynthia said. "But that was the first time I was in EDU. The next time he made me realize everyone looks at themselves on a shitty day and wishes they were different."

Julia set her knitting aside, moving around in her chair like her bones ached. "I was sixty-four pounds the last time I blacked out—I didn't wake up for twenty-two days. It was crazy. I mean, I kept hurting myself even when I was dying."

She stared at her walker with a kind of quiet shame. "Now I'm stuck with this for who knows how long? When I woke up I knew I didn't want to be one of those pathetic people who becomes her disease. I knew I wanted to live."

Bones glanced at her sideways. She frowned at her last five minutes of stitches and began ripping them out. Then she looked up at him and smiled. You could almost swim in her eyes they were so clear and blue. When she went back to her knitting he let thoughts of Alice fill him up. His insides swelled, like he was drowning in this daydream of pleasant pain.

Thirteen days had passed since Alice had run away. But he didn't know how long she'd been in a coma. Would she wake up slowly? Or all at once? One thing he knew for sure, Alice would rather die than be stuck with a walker and not able to dance.

Ramon drained his coffee, crushed his cup, and picked up the pamphlet. "Take what works for you and leave the rest," he said. "And keep coming back."

Bones looked at Julia who looked back at him. She pushed her walker across the carpet, her pack pulling down a shoulder. Her eyes fell on Bones again, like they had a little secret. "If you're having a problem, someone will have a solution. Usually me."

Bones couldn't say anything back.

Lard had tacked his poetry assignment on his bulletin board. It seemed a perfect, though an admittedly flippant way, to follow Mary Oliver's opening lines, *One day you finally knew what you had to do, and began, though the voices around you kept shouting*…Dr. Chu required everyone to finish the line.

Lard had written, *Sure I could shout back if I wanted to and be louder than everyone else because I'm bigger and could shatter a wine glass with a sneeze if I wanted to but I just don't care that much anymore about what people think of me.*

Bones took out his journal and chewed on the end of his pencil. He'd never come up with anything as real as that, and not just because he still cared too much about what people thought of him. He'd never known anyone as comfortable in his own skin as Lard.

…*Voices around you kept shouting*…Bones knew only too well about voices. They'd been running the same circles inside his head for years, starving little dogs trapped in a boneyard. It was time to let them out to explore the neighborhood.

*One day you finally knew what you had to do*…Instead of finishing the line, he got up and went to the window and began shouting until his ears rang and his throat was raw and the voices were little more than a leaky valve. He smiled to himself, then laughter kicked in. He laughed so hard he was coughing up fur balls of irony when Unibrow stuck his head in the doorway.

"This is no-joke Tuesday," he said.

Bones dabbed his sore eye with his sleeve.

"Er, just kidding."

"I figured."

"Gumbo says dinner's in the kitchen tonight," Unibrow said. "Don't be late."

After Unibrow unplugged his bulk from the doorway, Bones hit the bathroom and splashed cold water on his face. Instead of weak, pale, and helpless, he thought the shiner made him look like a formidable fighter. A great year-book picture.

Dinner in the kitchen could only mean one thing: Dr. Chu wanted to evaluate their cooking skills. If anything he was surprised it hadn't happened sooner and hoped the recipes wouldn't be too complicated. He passed through the dayroom, catching up to Sarah and Mary-Jane, strolling with their arms linked. He wondered why girls were always doing something weird with their hair. Sarah's bangs were spiked, like porcupine quills.

"Who won the fight?" she asked.

Bones knew she meant his black eye. He stepped in front of her and opened the door to the stairs. "You wouldn't believe it if I told you."

Mary-Jane stalled, her knuckles embedded in a mass of hips. "What's wrong with the elevator?"

Bones took a stutter step; the word *elevator* was loaded with meaning. "I bet you've never gone this way," he said.

"Why would we?"

"Because it's against the rules," he said.

That was good enough for them.

"Dr. Chu probably wants us to document our relationship with a dead animal before and after eating it," Sarah said like she'd rather lap gravy from a pig trough.

Mary-Jane panted, taking the stairs slowly. "Maybe it isn't about cooking." Clearly the idea was beneath her. "Maybe it's some sort of art project. We made gingerbread men in kindergarten. Stupid Harry Pitts bit the head off my cookie."

"Psycho."

"I cried."

Lard met them at the door to the kitchen in a puffy chef's hat.

"Nice look," Sarah said.

"You're about to eat your words," Lard said.

Teresa stepped up in a floral sundress. "Welcome to Chez Kowlesky."

The kitchen could have been a four-star restaurant—if it weren't for the counters, sinks, cupboards, stove, ovens, fridge, and blinding fluorescent lights. Bones wondered if anyone else noticed there didn't seem to be any cooking going on. The stove was off. No pots or pans or the usual steamy chaos. No messy bowls or whisks lying around. And the room was fifteen degrees cooler than normal.

"Think I'll make myself a peanut butter and jelly sandwich and call it a night," Mary-Jane said.

Lard hung out by the door greeting Dr. Chu, Nancy, and Unibrow. The latter read the room quickly and excused himself with a Neanderthal grunt. Dr. Chu fingered his tie. "Is dinner being delivered?" As if Lard would order take-out.

Elsie and Nicole came in, short of breath. "Sorry, we forgot we were meeting in here."

Lard opened a cupboard and reached for a stack of plates. Chip-free china, not the usual scratched plastic. He lined everyone up in front of the counter. Bones was sandwiched between Mary-Jane and Nicole. He knew he should've been nervous about whatever was about to happen—something out of the ordinary obviously. But he took a plate like everybody else, trusting his roommate.

Before anyone could make another smart-ass remark Lard opened the dishwasher, lunging backward when steam poured out. "Dr. Chu?" Lard handed over a pair of tongs with a flourish. "Please take your dinner out of the dishwasher."

Dr. Chu squinted skeptically at packets of foil winking

at him from the top rack. Each one had a name on it. The others fell over themselves laughing before taking turns with the tongs. Bones busted up too. Lard had actually done it.

Bones knew dinner wasn't about Lard showing off what he'd learned in the kitchen. He could've poured ketchup over tater tots and the girls would've dropped to the floor and kissed his boots. But Lard wanted to do something special for his friends.

"Each packet is its own meal," Lard explained. "Prepared according to your own individual nutritional requirements. All natural, steamed in their own juices."

Mary-Jane chewed the end of her braid and eyed her packet skeptically.

"Come on, this is supposed to be fun," Lard said. "You can't fuck up foil. Just rip it open."

"He's right." Dr. Chu opened his packet with the care of a surgeon. His dinner glistened in its own salty gel. SPAM. "You're not being graded."

Bones unfolded his foil giving the salmon and garden vegetables the admiration they deserved. He may not have been the first person to get the significance of what was happening, but he was the first to say it.

"Do you realize what we're witnessing?" he said. "Lard's a guy in an Eating Disorder program who's more focused on cooking than eating. Seems like such a person should be ready to go home."

Dr. Chu said, "Or well on his way."

Lard shrugged, embarrassed. He told everyone how he came up with the idea. "No added calories, like stir-fry for instance, which uses oil," he said. "And no oil splatter-burns on your clothes. I used full cycle. No soap."

Nicole, Sarah, and Mary-Jane ate their pork tenderloin silently like three starving refuges. Elsie ate like a three-hundred pound bouncer.

"Stir-fry only takes a few minutes," Sarah said. "Our dishwasher at home takes forty-five minutes. That's a long time to wait when you're hungry."

"I'm working on that," Lard said.

"You can recycle the foil," Teresa said.

Bones couldn't help but think about Alice. She would've loved this more than anyone. He knew the others were aware of her absence and missed her snarky remarks. They had to be worried about her too. But talking about Alice right now would be a downer. Besides this was Lard's show.

Bones finished his salmon thinking about her treasonous body and reckless mind. He thought of warm days and stolen nights on the roof. He thought of driving down the Santa Monica freeway with the windows down and music cranked. He thought of his hands on her and her hands on him and ten blissful minutes in the elevator with all its hopes, dreams, and promises.

He thought that it was just all so amazing and wonderful and unreal and he knew he'd never let it go.

# 35

Bones spent his first few days home with his family cleaning out his room. His sister bagged up sweats for the Salvation Army. The library took his old *Weight Watchers* magazines. The hardest part was getting rid of his dumbbells and digital scales. He told himself this was a good way to start over without moving to China and taking up ping-pong. It pissed him off that he still felt so uneasy at the dining room table with his family. It wasn't just because he thought eating like a normal person would make him fat. *Yes, it was. No, it wasn't.* The argument raged on between every molecule in his brain. He'd mistakenly believed that six weeks in the loony foodie bin would erase this type of thinking.

"Eating an apple fills me up," he told his sister one afternoon. "And being full makes me feel fat."

"Do you want to throw up?" she asked.

"No."

"Power down laxatives?"

"Nuh-uh."

"Do jumping jacks in the middle of the night?"

"I have a stash of red M&Ms in my nightstand," he admitted.

Jill punched him playfully in the arm. "Cut yourself some slack, weirdo," she said with a crooked smile. "It's not like you're still wearing those dumb gloves!"

True.

And he hadn't missed an outpatient meeting since checking out of the program a month ago. He'd even gotten together with some of the ex-patients away from the hospital. Sometimes they went to the movies as a group; other times they hung out at Julia's house playing Story Cubes or Bananagrams.

..........

Bones tried not to call Nancy more than twice a week. She usually called back within an hour. His questions were always in the same desperate tone. "Have you heard anything about Alice? Has she woken up yet?"

"Sorry, she's still in a coma," Nancy said the first time he called. Her voice quivered. But the next time she answered his questions with a steady patience.

"Is it like being asleep or unconscious?" he'd asked.

"There's some level of consciousness as long as she's breathing."

"Can she hear people in her room?"

"We assume a person in a coma can hear," she'd said. "Hearing is usually the last sensory faculty to go."

"There isn't anything new," Nancy said the last time. "Except her parents transferred her to a hospital out of state that specializes in comatose care."

Bones concentrated to slow his breathing. "If they're experts, then they'll be able to help her, right?"

Her pause crackled through the airwaves. When she spoke it sounded like her heart was crumbling onto the cold linoleum floor. "The longer she's unconscious, the worse the prognosis," she said softly. "Sorry, I wish it were different."

For the first time since Bones left the hospital he wanted to lock himself in his room and exercise until he passed out. And that's what he told Lard the next afternoon when Lard picked him up in the Doodle. He was doing fifty in a thirty-five zone. Music engulfed the car like Alice was controlling the radio.

"You think I haven't wanted to order a dozen pizzas in the middle of the night?" Lard said. "Scarf them down alone in the dark in front of the Food Channel?"

"You still think about that?"

Lard shot him a look. Then he reached into the ashtray and pulled out a roach, twisting the tiny end like he was strangling it. "Let's face it, man. Some days are just not all that great. You know why I don't call nine-one-one-PIZZA? Because everything doesn't have to be a fucking soap opera. Sometimes a person just has to work things out on his own."

"I still love her." Bones had to say it, because Lard was

the only person who truly understood what had gone on in the hospital. Though sometimes he wondered if he ever really knew Alice or the world she'd created for herself where decisions were made without regard to consequences.

"Do you ever think—" Bones paused, pulling the seatbelt away from his chest, letting it slap back with force, hating the universe for making it impossible to undo the past. "What will happen if she doesn't wake up?"

Lard hit the brakes and turned into a gravel parking lot. "Yeah, man. She'll be dead."

*Thanks.*

"I'm going to keep calling Nancy," Bones said. "And finish writing CRAP. I'm going to come up with an ending that'll give life to that dark place Alice is in now."

Lard turned off the engine, grabbed his keys, and grunted his way out of the front seat. "Ducks are waiting."

Bones picked up the bag of stale bread and followed Lard, weaving around families who were squeezing out the last days of summer barbequing, tossing Frisbees, playing horseshoes.

Teresa waved from a picnic table where she sat with Julia and Ramon.

Lard waved back. "She's one of the reasons I can't be a self-centered asshole the rest of my life."

Bones got it.

Julia scooted off the bench and he took in the picture: her shredded jean skirt and a tank top the color of a raspberry snow cone. She limped awkwardly down the path toward them. "Guess what?" she asked, all smiles.

Bones noticed right away, but he couldn't say it. There was too much below the surface of what he was seeing.

"Ditched the walker," she said, impatient for an answer.

Bones clutched the bag of bread and pushed ahead of Lard. Halfway to the table he let the bag fly.

Julia caught it mid-air and took aim back at him. "Ready?"

"Yeah." He was ready.

# From Lard's New Cookbook: Dishwasher Salmon

## INGREDIENTS:

**4** (6-oz.) salmon fillets

**4** Tbsp. freshly squeezed lime juice

**1** Tbsp. olive oil

Salt and freshly ground black pepper to taste

## DIRECTIONS:

Cut two 12-inch square sheets of heavy-duty aluminum foil.

Grease the shiny side of the foil with oil. Place two fillets side by side on each square and fold up the outer edges.

Drizzle 1 Tbsp. lime juice over each fillet. Season with salt and pepper.

Fold and pinch the aluminum foil to create a watertight seal around each pair of fillets.

Place fish packets on the top rack of dishwasher.

Run packets through the entire wash-and-dry cycle, approximately 50 minutes.

When the cycle is complete, invite friends into the kitchen and ask them to take their dinner out of the dishwasher.

# The Truth about Eating Disorders

**THE ALLIANCE FOR EATING DISORDERS AWARENESS STATES:**

Eating disorders currently affect approximately 25 million Americans, in which 25% are men.

Anorexia is the third-most common chronic illness among adolescents.

Eating disorders have the highest mortality rate of any mental illness.

**ACCORDING TO THE NATIONAL ASSOCIATION OF ANOREXIA NERVOSA AND ASSOCIATED DISORDERS (ANAD):**

The mortality rate associated with anorexia nervosa is 12 times higher than the death rate of all causes of death for females 15–24 years old.

Ninety-five percent of those with eating disorders are between the ages of 12 and 25.

Five to ten percent of anorexics die within ten years after contracting the disease; 18–20% of anorexics will be dead after twenty years; only 50% ever fully recover.

**FOR HELP:**

The ANAD website (www.anad.org) lists eating disorder support groups by state. A free brochure, "How to Help a Friend," is also available to download.

The ANAD helpline (630-577-1330) is open Monday through Friday, 9:00 a.m.–5:00 p.m. central time. ANAD also has an email address, anadhelp@anad.org.

**ADDITIONAL RESOURCES:**

The National Eating Disorders Association (NEDA) www.nationaleatingdisorders.org

The National Association for Males with Eating Disorders Inc. (NAMED) namedinc.org

**Sherry Shahan** is the author of more than thirty-five books. When not writing, she can be found in a ballet studio or competing in a West Coast Swing dance contest. She holds an MFA in Writing for Children and Young Adults from Vermont College of Fine Arts. *Skin and Bones* was inspired by a short story she wrote called "Iris and Jim" that appeared in literary journals and anthologies around the world. Sherry lives on the Central Coast of California.